TEN YEARS FROM NOW

—— ❖ ——

KRISTEN GRAFTON

COTTAGE HOUSE PUBLISHING

My ultimate goal upon completion of this Master's degree program is to pursue a Ph.D. program in pursuit of becoming a history professor. Being a lifelong researcher, learner, and educator would fulfill multiple passions of mine. The classes I am currently taking in my undergraduate program have prepared me to continue this pursuit of higher education. Boston University would provide unique opportunities of study for me. As the heart of much of U.S. history, I would have the chance to study American history from the plentiful primary sources and architecture available in the city of Boston. Boston University is the ideal place for me to continue my studies because it has superior professors, elite classes, and geographical relevance to my field. I greatly look forward to further developing and enriching my own knowledge and education, and I feel that Boston is the right place for me to do so.

1

The printer turned on suddenly and started spitting out papers, startling me out of my daze. I'd had my laptop open for about fifteen minutes, but I'd mostly been staring blankly at the wall. With no one else in the faculty lounge, it had been quiet, and after four periods of attempting to teach boisterous high school juniors about the Civil War, the relative peace was welcome.

I knew someone would be here in a few moments to collect whatever it is they printed—something that was clearly multiple pages and stapled, so it was going to take a while—so I tried to refocus on my work. I was behind on my thesis, and I had only myself to blame: I had the absolute gall to assign a two-page essay in a *history* class. My students had whined at the time "this isn't English class," and I had rebuked them for their poor work ethics, but now that I had graded fifty of those essays and gotten behind on my own work, their ill-constructed teenager logic was starting to make a lot of sense.

Completing a Master's degree in history had been a goal of mine for several years now, but I never imagined myself doing it while teaching full-time. I'd had lofty aspirations of going to graduate school straight out of college, working on my Master's while teaching undergraduate classes, maybe traveling for some more complex research, and then landing some professorship position at a top university. I definitely hadn't thought I'd be twenty-eight years old teaching moody high schoolers and struggling to finish writing a paper—something that used to be easy for me to do—but life rarely works out the way we plan.

The door opened, and I was surprised to see the principal Mr. Quentin walk in. He likely was not responsible for the excessive printing currently taking place, and he did not often darken the door of the faculty lounge. I thought he was afraid that too many teachers would bring up too many problems for him to fix, so he just avoided it all together.

"Ah, April, there you are," he said. "I've been looking for you. Do you have a moment?"

No, I don't, I wanted to say, but obviously I didn't. "Sure, Mr. Quentin, what do you need?"

He pulled up a chair from a nearby table despite the fact that the table I was sitting at had several empty chairs and sat backwards on the chair, resting his arms across the back of the chair. Mr. Quentin was one of those bosses who was quite a bit older than his employees and aware of it, so he tried to be "cool" and "hip" to relate to us, but, unfortunately for him, he was also the kind of boss who felt so uniquely "adult" and authoritarian that one could hardly call him by his first name—he was always just "Mr. Quentin."

"We're in the process of planning the class reunions this year, and I understand that your reunion is one of the main reunions this year. Class of 2014, right?"

"Yes, that's right."

"That must be very exciting. Are you looking forward to it?" He pushed his glasses up his nose, but they slid down immediately.

"I guess so."

I'd been one of those weird freaks who hadn't hated high school. I had actually kind of liked it. I'd had good friends, and I'd taken classes and participated in activities I enjoyed, so I wasn't dreading my reunion. I hadn't thought I'd ever be back at that same school as a teacher, but it wasn't unwelcome. Still, I thought there was something universal about the dread surrounding a high school reunion. Would you live up to or surpass the expectations everyone else had for you? Did everyone else even *have* expectations of you, or were you a nothing? Would it be fun to see everyone again, or would you just be reminded of what you didn't like about high school or have your classmates' success rubbed in your face?

"Well, I wanted to ask for your help. Typically, the class president of each class helps us plan the reunion, but your class president, uh, Emily?"

"Emma," I said. "Emma Wilson."

He snapped his fingers. "Yes, Emma Wilson. Well, she's still overseas right now, so she isn't available to help us. She sent us some ideas for activities, but she won't make it to the reunion."

Right after college, Emma had moved to Europe, and she'd been traveling ever since. I didn't remember what she studied, but it had something to do with art or culture or something like that, and she had landed some kind of dream job overseas. She had definitely won the high school reunion success jackpot, so it was a shame she would miss her chance to show off.

Mr. Quentin continued, "We need someone local to help us prepare for the reunion—plan activities, make reservations, stuff like that."

Oh no. He wanted my help. "What about Ryan Bennings? He was vice president."

"And he's confirmed that he's coming, but he won't be in town until a couple of days before the reunion. He's offered his help with the mechanics of the actual events, but he won't be able to help until then."

Ryan Bennings was coming? I hadn't seen him since the day we graduated. He was definitely someone I'd very much look forward to seeing again.

"Could you help us out? We really want someone from the class to help. And I hear you were in student goverment."

"I was the class secretary," I said, "and that was really just because I had a fast typing speed. Seriously, I wasn't really that involved."

"Still, that's involvement."

"Mr. Quentin, I'd love to help, but I've already got a lot on my plate. I'm a little behind on my coursework, and AP exam prep is always time-consuming."

"The AP exams are many months away."

"Sure, but I have good pass rates because I work toward them with my students all year."

"Ms. Corwin," he began, folding his hands, and I knew he was serious when he used my last name instead of my first, "I have all the confidence in the world that you can manage your work responsibilities. You're a very effective teacher. And you won't be alone in the planning. The administrative office staff will help you out. I'm not asking you to take over the whole reunion, but we need someone who will help us make some major decisions. Can I count on you?"

And there it was: the phrase I couldn't say no to. The people pleaser in me wouldn't allow it.

"Sure, I'll help out."

He slammed his hand on the table. "Fantastic! Oh, I'm so glad. Okay, I will forward Emma Wilson's emails to you so that you can sift through the suggestions she had. I'll also send you Ryan Bennings's emails. He said he would be happy to coordinate with someone and help talk through ideas until he gets here. I'll let him know to expect to hear from you."

"Oh, okay." Ryan Bennings. I was going to work on this with Ryan Bennings?

Get it together, April. I wasn't in high school anymore. I could talk to Ryan now.

"If you need financial information at any point for reservations, just let Diane in the office know. She can forward the information."

"Is there a date for the reunion?" In the back of my mind, I was vaguely aware that I received an email about it, but I had forgotten to RSVP and therefore didn't remember what the date was.

"The weekend of October 20th. We're planning events that whole weekend. Obviously Friday night, we'll be here for the homecoming football game, but you can decide what you want to plan for Saturday and Sunday. Just let the class know as soon as you do so that they know what to expect."

October 20th?? That was much sooner than I thought. It was also only a month before my thesis was due. What had I gotten myself into?

"I'm so elated you've agreed to help with this, April," Mr. Quentin said. Of course, now that I had agreed, we were back to first names. "Let me know if you need anything."

Administrators liked to say that, but I wasn't sure they always meant it.

"Thanks, I will."

He pushed his glasses up again—a futile action—and walked out the door with a smile and a wave.

I looked back at my screen, where no new words had appeared in the last thirty minutes, and sighed as the bell rang for sixth period to start.

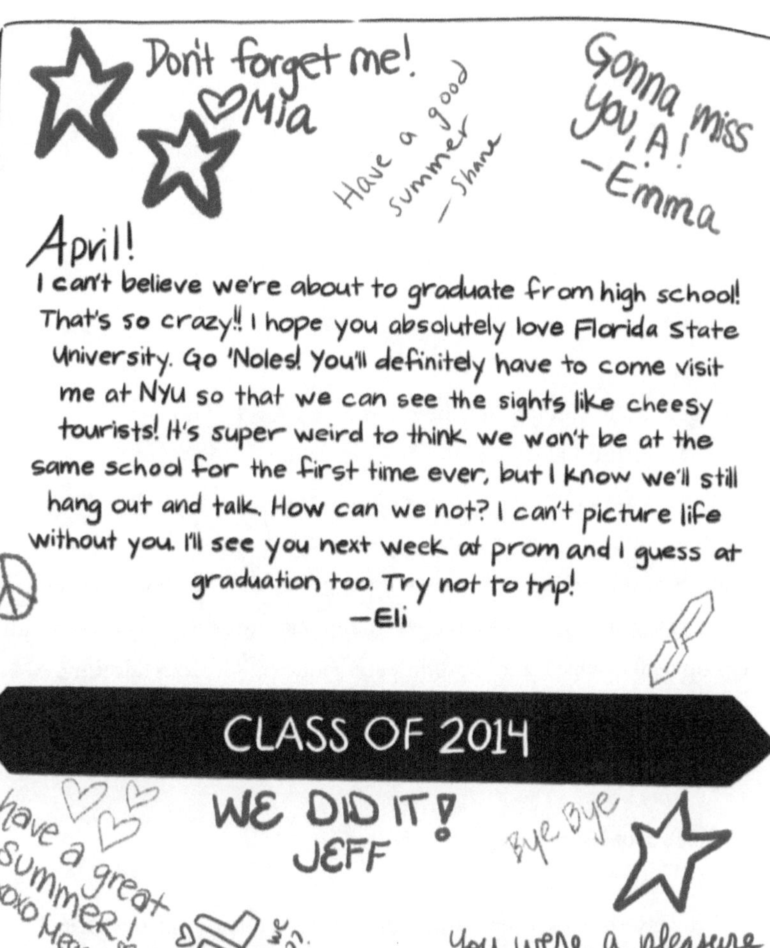
Don't forget me!
♡Mia

Have a good summer
-Shane

Gonna miss you, A!
-Emma

April!
I can't believe we're about to graduate from high school! That's so crazy!! I hope you absolutely love Florida State University. Go 'Noles! You'll definitely have to come visit me at NYU so that we can see the sights like cheesy tourists! It's super weird to think we won't be at the same school for the first time ever, but I know we'll still hang out and talk. How can we not? I can't picture life without you. I'll see you next week at prom and I guess at graduation too. Try not to trip!
—Eli

CLASS OF 2014

have a great summer!
xoxo Megan

WE DID IT!
JEFF

Bye Bye

APRIL
Isn't it cray cray we are graduating??? Promise we will stay in touch
-Amanda

You were a pleasure to have in class. Best of luck in college!
Warmly, Mrs. Gabler

2

— . —

"You're kidding," my best friend Paige said. "Girl, you've got to learn to say no."

I avoided eye contact by stirring my chai tea latte obsessively, ignoring how loudly the ice was clanking around in the glass. Paige didn't really have time to talk right now—it was a busy time of the day at the donut shop she owned—so she was filling out budget reports on her laptop while I talked, and she didn't even notice my anxious fidgeting.

"I know, but how was I supposed to say no to this?"

"Like this: 'no.' See? It's easy."

"It's my boss."

"He's a lot less scary than Mr. Patterson."

I snorted. "True."

Mr. Patterson had been the principal of River Glen Academy when we were students there, and Paige wasn't kidding. He was scarier than the detention guy in *The Breakfast Club*.

"Aren't you supposed to be finishing your thesis project?"

I nodded.

Paige sighed. "April, come on. You do not have time for this."

"Well, it's already done, so I guess I'm just going to have to figure it out."

Paige tucked a short blonde lock of hair behind her ear, and it immediately popped back out. Our senior year of high school, she cut her hair short a week after she took her senior pictures, and she'd had it that way ever since. It was her act of rebellion. Her mom really wanted her to have long hair in her senior pictures, and I guess she got what she wanted, but I always laughed when I saw her senior picture—it just didn't look like her anymore.

"So are you an island planning this? Is anyone helping?"

"They said the office staff will help." I paused, unsure if I wanted to tell Paige this next detail or not, but I figured she'd find out eventually. "Ryan Bennings is supposed to help me, too."

"RYAN BENNINGS?" she shouted a little too loudly, so I shushed her. "I thought he moved to Boston."

"He did. He's coming into town for the reunion, but Mr. Quentin said that Ryan was willing to help from a distance. He's giving him my email."

"Oh my gosh, it's fate."

"Shut up, it is not."

She didn't hear me, and her eyes sparkled with mischief. "Oh my goodness, this is like a Hallmark movie. You'll get a second chance. You can still marry the high school quarterback."

"Don't make it weird. Besides, he's not a quarterback anymore. He's an accountant."

"Did you look him up on LinkedIn? Stalker."

"It's normal to use LinkedIn at this point in our lives, you know."

She flitted her hand at me. "Sure, whatever. Okay, so other than Ryan, what other help do you have?"

"Emma Wilson sent over some of her ideas. I have to go through those."

"That's it?"

"I guess," I said.

"April, that's not good. You're going to end up planning this whole thing alone."

"Well, I was hoping that maybe you'd pitch in?"

"No, no, no," she said, waving her arms in an x-shape in front of her face. "See? I can say it, unlike you. Besides, I have no desire to return to high school. I don't even know if I'm going to the reunion."

"What? You have to! I can't go to this thing by myself. We're the only people still in town."

"You won't be alone. Maybe Ryan will be your date."

"You're not going to let it go, are you?"

"Definitely not. I plan to give a speech at your wedding."

"Oh, so now I'm marrying him?"

"Wasn't that on your dream board or something in high school?"

I felt my cheeks get hot. "Sure, when I was seventeen. Things are different now."

"We'll see."

I leaned forward. "Please come to the reunion."

"Fine," she said without looking up from her computer.

"And please help me with this."

She groaned and looked up at me in annoyance, but I folded my hands and mouthed "please," and she sighed. "Fine. If you're drowning and think you'll fail out of graduate school and all of your students will fail their exams and you're a failure at life, then I'll help you."

"Glad to know what your priorities are."

***

Paige had to do some inventory reports, so she ducked into the back, leaving me alone in my usual corner table by the window. I liked this spot because I wasn't readily visible from the street, but I could still people watch or just look out the window. The River Glen downtown street was really beautiful. It was one of those old historic streets that you only found in small towns. None of the buildings matched, and that was kind of endearing. Some looked colonial, some modern, and others were some kind of strange mish-mosh in between, and that made each one unique.

I used to hate this street when I was growing up. It felt fake, like a movie set designed to depict some charm that was really just a cover-up for peeling paint, shuttered foreclosures, and lack of money for refurbishments. I had dreamed of the day I could get out, move to a big city with a real downtown that consisted of more than just one street with nothing but Mom and Pop shops. That dream still lingered in the back of my mind, but I didn't hate this street anymore.

The ice in my chai tea latte had melted long ago, but I still sipped it absent-mindedly, hoping the caffeine would at least inspire some words that I desperately needed to write. I came here most days after school to work because if I went home, I would get distracted too easily by the laundry I'd put off, the dishes that were piling up in the sink, and the to-do list on my fridge, but today, even the change of scenery wasn't helping.

I typed out a few sentences then immediately deleted them. I'd done this multiple times. A few months ago, I didn't even know what my thesis would be about. Having to write a fifty-page paper was daunting—still was—and no idea seemed good enough to sustain that much research and work. When I finally settled on an analysis of primary sources found during the Civil War from Union sympathizers living in the South, it at least felt possible. I kind of liked the idea because it felt more like reading stories or old-timey gossip instead of actual research, so it wasn't a lack of passion that was inhibiting this project. I knew exactly what I wanted to write too, having written a detailed outline months ago. I just couldn't seem to shake the feeling that every sentence I wrote was terrible and would result in my failing out of my entire degree program.

I couldn't help but think that this would have been so much easier if I had done this sooner when I could have worked as a graduate teaching assistant for basically no money at a time when I didn't have bills to pay. I would have had a lot more free time. Fitting in research and writing around grading papers and attending football games was a lot harder than I thought it would be.

Paige had bought one of those annoying chimes that rang every time someone opened the door of the coffee shop, so every so often, my thoughts were interrupted by an irritating high-pitched jingle, and it was the kind of sound you couldn't ignore, so you compulsively stared at the person walking through the door. It was the kind of thing that annoyed me when I was the one walking through the door and drawing stares, but I couldn't stop myself from doing the same.

This time of day, usually I saw some students walk in or locals that I'd known my whole life but didn't know their first names. Occasionally it was a UPS driver with a delivery for Paige. Rarely, it was an out-of-towner who was just traveling through and expected a small-town coffee shop to have the exact same menu as a Starbucks.

I didn't expect to see Eli Forrester walk through the door. Something about the way he walked was so familiar, like I'd be able to tell it was Eli without seeing his face. He always had kind of casual sway to the way he walked, like he was never rushing to get anywhere, always on his own timetable but never late. He always had one hand in the pocket of his pants and one hanging loosely but snapping, a nervous habit that he'd had as long as I'd known him. His sandy brown hair was cut short, as always, a habit leftover from his naval officer father. His muddled blue eyes still looked like they were hiding secrets—not in a bad way, but like he had a depth of knowledge that most people didn't have.

He ordered coffee from the girl working the counter, and I was sorry that Paige wasn't there. She would have liked to see him. I thought about calling him over, but somehow, it felt unnatural. How long had it been since we'd spoken? We used to be inseparable, and now I felt like I was looking at a stranger even though I knew where he had scars on his hands from climbing the trees in his backyard, and how he always laughed with the kind of wild abandon that only children laugh with because adults censor their innate joy, and how he snapped his fingers when he walked even though his fingers were oddly idle now.

He sat down at a table near me, but he was facing the other way, and it felt awkward to call out to him. What if he didn't hear me, and then everyone around me would be looking at me strangely? He seemed absorbed in whatever he was reading on his phone. When he took the lid off of his coffee, I smelled the familiar smell of hazelnut flavored creamer that he always used to order. I guessed some things never changed.

I tried to focus back on my own work, but if I hadn't been able to focus before, I certainly couldn't focus now. Not with Eli sitting nearby. I considered just leaving and going home, giving up on making any kind of progress, but just as I was mentally arguing with myself over leaving, Eli turned around to pick up something he had dropped, and when he saw me, he smiled.

"April?"

"Eli. I thought that was you."

He gestured to the empty seat across from him at his table. "Come join me."

I took the seat, and when I looked up at him, I was startled by how much like himself he looked. I didn't know why I expected him to look different—I guessed I thought time or age would have changed him—but he was still just Eli with the same wide smile and deep eyes.

"What are you doing in town?" I asked.

He gave me kind of strange, curious look and chuckled. "I'm here for the reunion."

Oh my gosh, duh, stupid question, April. I couldn't believe that was the first thing I thought to say. Why else would he have been here?

"That's still a few weeks away. You're kind of early, don't you think?"

He shrugged and leaned back, keeping a hand on his coffee cup. "I finished my residency a little while ago, so I thought I'd take a little bit of time off to help my parents out since they're downsizing, and I don't want my dad to lift too many heavy boxes."

I had heard that the Forresters were selling their house. The news made me kind of sad. Eli and I had spent so much time in that backyard as kids.

"I didn't think dentists had to do residencies."

"Not for general dentistry," Eli said, "but I'm going for orthodontics, so I just finished a two-year residency."

Orthodontist. Eli Forrester was an orthodontist. That was hard to picture. There was something about your high school friends that if you didn't see them regularly, in your mind, they were always sixteen years old, copying your history homework they forgot to do or wearing a silly outfit during spirit week. It was hard to think of them as adults. Honestly, it was even hard to think of myself as an adult.

"That's great," I said, but I was aware that it sounded lackluster. If Eli noticed, he didn't call me on it. I did notice that he was snapping his fingers again.

"So what about you? I knew you were back in town, but I haven't heard what you're doing."

Not back in town. I never really left. I went to college, but this place sucked me right back in.

"I teach history at River Glen Academy."

"No way!" he said, and it sounded far more genuine than I had. "I can totally see you doing that. I know you always wanted to teach."

Not high schoolers, I thought to myself. I had always wanted to teach, but I had imagined being a professor teaching college students or maybe even graduate students.

"I never pictured myself back at our high school, though," I said, and it was something true I could say without sounding bitter.

"Is that weird?"

"Very weird. I'm in Mr. Tucker's old classroom."

"Ew," he said, laughing. "Does it still smell like his nasty cologne?"

I laughed, too. "No, thank goodness. But he left behind all of his posters."

"Oh, so you obviously hung them all up, right?"

I was laughing even harder now. "Absolutely not. Why did he ever have posters of the founding fathers as members of NSYNC?"

"I think he was trying to be relatable."

"It didn't work."

We were both laughing, and I was aware that we were being kind of loud since there weren't many people in here, but it was nice to see Eli again. It was always easy with Eli to have fun. He had always made me laugh.

Having exhausted the Mr. Tucker gag, we both seemed stuck in a lull without an idea of what to talk about. The silence made me uncomfortable, so I searched for something, anything, to end it.

"Have you seen Paige yet?"

"No. I'll have to catch her later. Obviously, I was hoping she'd be here, but—"

"She is, but she's in the back working. I can go get her if—"

"No, that's okay. I'm in town for a while."

"Any chance you'd be willing to help me plan our reunion?"

As soon as the words were out of my mouth, I regretted them, mostly because of the shocked expression on his face. Did I really just ask for his help? He had literally just told me he's here to help his parents. He probably didn't have time.

"You're planning the reunion?"

"Yes, I mean, no, I mean— Emma is in Italy or Germany or something, and my boss basically roped me into it, and I couldn't say no, and—"

He took my floundering hand in his, stopping my babbling in its tracks. How many times must he have done this over the years whenever I got myself worked up and started ranting or babbling, but I never used to wish he wouldn't let go, and I found myself wishing that.

"Sure, I'll help," he said, still smiling.

"Really? Because you don't have to. I'm just kind of panicking because I have a ton of work to do, and now I'm stuck with this."

"Don't worry about it. I've got the time. Let me help."

I sighed. "Thank you. I kind of forced Paige into helping me, but she really wasn't excited about it. When she finds out you agreed to help, she might just give you free coffee for bailing her out."

"Hey, I'll take the free coffee."

His hand were still on mine, and it felt like we'd gotten to that point where it had gone on too long but neither of us knew how to end it.

"Ryan Bennings is supposed to help, too, but he won't be in town until closer to the reunion."

For whatever reason, that snapped the moment like a twig. Eli gently let go of my hand and shifted in his seat.

"Ryan, huh? I'm surprised he's showing up."

"Why are you surprised? He was our vice president."

"Only because it was a popularity contest, and everyone knows football players win those every time in high school."

He said it jokingly, but there was something bitter behind his tone.

"Well, anyway, I'm grateful for the help."

The smile was back. "Happy to help." He checked his watch and sat up straighter. "Hey, I've got to head out, but give me call and let me know what you need. My number is still the same. Okay? See you later."

He walked out, and I watched him leave. It felt bold of him to assume that I still knew his number or still have it saved in my phone, but of course, I had both. I pulled up the contact, and it was an old picture of him from college—probably the last time we had really talked beyond wishing each other a happy birthday on Facebook each year. I wanted to replace it, but I didn't have a new picture. I looked up his LinkedIn profile, but that picture was too corporate. It didn't look like him. He still looked the same.

Dear Diary~*~

Do you ever get tired of me writing about Quinn Pendleton? I guess not, being an inanimate object and all, but I think that sometimes I get tired of writing about her.

It's nothing new. Just Quinn being Quinn. It probably shouldn't bother me as much as it does. I should just let it go and not let her consume my thoughts and feelings all the time, but it's hard not to focus on her when she makes herself so focusable. Is that a word?

My mom says she's just insecure, that she targets girls like me because I'm prettier or smarter or nicer or more popular. I think that's ridiculous. I might be smarter or nicer than her, but I'm definitely not prettier, and more popular? It's like Mom forgot what high school is like. The smart girl who studies all the time instead of going to parties is never more popular than the cheer captain. That feels absurd even to write.

It's not even like I'm getting bullied. No one's shoving me into lockers or stealing my lunch money. Nobody's "accidentally" spilling soda all over my white shirt. This isn't an '80's rom-com. Mom says I could call it bullying to the principal, but I'm not going to cause a whole scene over some snide comments about being a teacher's pet or subtle laughs when I change during gym class. It's just not worth the aftermath that would follow.

Mom says girls like Quinn never win in the real world, but that doesn't help me now, does it? In high school, the Quinns always win, and don't people always say that high school never really ends? Doesn't that mean Quinn will always win?

Aside from the usual Quinn drama, I guess today was a good day. I helped Eli write his speech since he decided to run for class vice president. So far, he's unopposed. I hope it stays that way. He really wants to win.

I guess I can't put off my essay any longer. It's due tomorrow, and I still haven't finished the last paragraph.

 ~*~April  

3

— • —

"And this is our main ballroom," my tour guide Tom said, gesturing widely toward the room. "This is where we could hold the main event. It's plenty large enough to suit a group of your size."

Emma had suggested the local Marriott as an option for the main reunion event, so I booked a walk-through appointment, but the longer I was here, the more I felt like this was just not the right venue. It was a beautiful room, but it felt stiff and corporate. I felt like I should have been hosting a work conference here. I'd sat in many ballrooms just like this listening to speakers drone on about learning objectives and standards, and I couldn't picture trying to talk about dumb high school memories in the same room. Could one room be suitable to discuss student standardized test scores as well as prom after parties in someone's mom's basement?

"Are you planning on having dancing?" Tom asked, and I had to stop myself from laughing. I couldn't imagine that anyone would want to dance. We were almost thirty. We were professionals now. I certainly never participated in awkward group dances in high school, so I was not about to start now.

"No. We'll need tables for people to sit and eat and maybe some standing tables too for drinks."

"Would you like a plated dinner, or more like a buffet with small plates?"

"Small plates," I answered.

This conversation was pointless because I already knew I wasn't booking this venue, but I couldn't decide which was more rude: being nice and continuing this appointment only not to book and thus waste Tom's time or just walk out right now and insult him.

Tom's phone rang, so he answered it, and after a short conversation, he excused himself to run up to the front desk. I didn't mind the solitude, so I sat down at one of the staged tables layered with gaudy blue gauze and chuckled at it. I assumed that they thought blue would be good since that was one of River Glen's colors, but it was a weird shade of periwinkle instead of cobalt, and it loudly clashed with the partially maroon walls of the ballroom.

I refreshed my email several times in a row, hoping for an email—any email—to appear. I was waiting on advice from my major professor on my thesis, I had emailed Ryan, but hadn't heard back, and Mr. Quentin hadn't yet answered my questions about budget. Here I was at the Marriott, and I didn't even know if we could afford it since he hadn't given me a number. He had previously sworn that Ryan would have the budget numbers, but I didn't really know that I could trust that. Eli might have been a little harsh on Ryan the other day, but he hadn't been wrong that the election was a popularity contest. Ryan was not necessarily the best person for the job.

Eli had run for vice president back then. He was pretty mad that Ryan had won. Eli had put a lot of work into preparing his platform and his speeches. He had taken it way more seriously than Ryan ever had. That was probably when Ryan first started to get under his skin. I couldn't have blamed him back then, but it was hard to understand why he was still angry about it now. So much time had passed. Did it really matter anymore?

Tom poked his head back in and smiled. "Good news! It looks like someone else from your class arrived to help you plan."

I stood, confused. Paige was working, and Eli said that he was helping his parents today. Had he gotten a free moment and decided to drop in?

Before I could entertain any more positive thoughts of Paige or Eli walking through the door, I saw a familiar strut, a flip of flawlessly curled black hair, and a smile that gave me unwelcome flashbacks.

Quinn Pendleton was here.

"OMG, April!" Quinn threw her arms out for a hug, but in that really forced and fake way popular girls from high school always did. "It's been forever!"

I reluctantly accepted the hug because it would have been more trouble not to, and I resented the squeeze she gave me.

"How have you been?" she asked, hands still on my shoulders so I couldn't get away.

"Okay," I said. "Busy." I didn't feel obligated to share details of my life with Quinn.

Quinn Pendleton was a walking stereotype. She had been head cheerleader, dated the football quarterback (read: Ryan Bennings) for two years, married a stock broker immediately out of college and had a beautiful child that got the most unfortunate combination of features from her parents, but Quinn insisted that she was her "mini me."

She was also mean as a snake in high school, which felt like a requirement of her high school status.

"Oh my goodness, I know, I've been crazy busy, too," Quinn said, practically wiping her brow of imaginary sweat. "Did you hear that I opened my own salon?"

Of course I had. *Everyone* had heard. She basically inherited a salon from her mom's best friend, but she still liked to call herself an entrepreneur. Every so often, I stalked her on Facebook, usually prompted by her messaging me once or twice a year to sell me some product in her latest pyramid scheme. Quinn was the kind of Facebook friend you kept on your friends list not because you actually cared about her but because you wanted to hate-scroll and creep on her life, hoping it was a failure.

Quinn's pretty much never was.

"Yeah, how's that going?" I asked, mostly because I knew she was going to tell me anyway.

"Oh it's a lot, you know, but it's so rewarding seeing how happy clients are when they leave. I just love that I have such an important job, you know? I mean, what's more important than making women feel beautiful? I just can't think of anything more important."

I would have rather shaved my head bald than let Quinn touch a hair on my head.

She continued, "So how are things with you? I heard you're back at our alma mater. Good for you. I can't picture you anywhere else."

Why were people like Quinn so good at that? The comments that sounded nice if you looked at the words individually, but somehow they dripped with disdain and judgment. With condescension.

"It's been good," I said. "I've got a lot going on right now."

"Oh, I bet. Well, I am here to offer my help. Whatever you need. We want our reunion to be perfect, right? So I'm here to make sure everything is just right."

"What?"

"Well, I've been talking to Ryan, and since he won't be here until later, I offered to fill his shoes. I had no idea you were helping, but I'm still glad I offered."

Of course she had already talked to Ryan. She was probably hoping that he'd help her cheat on her husband.

"You really don't have to," I said, not because I didn't need the help but because I definitely didn't need *her* help.

"I'm already here. Besides, how are you going to plan all of this? Without Emma, I mean. I mean, we're all busy, but I think it's really important that I take some time away from all of my chaos to help you out."

I wanted to say no, to tell her to get lost, to tell her I had never and would never want her help, but my anxiety surrounding my un-finished thesis pounded in the back of my head louder than my own heartbeat, so I did what I had always done in high school: gave in.

"Sure, Quinn," I said, practically gritting my teeth. "Thanks for offering."

A flip of her hair. "Of course! I have to make sure the reunion is actually fabulous, you know?"

And there it was. "I wouldn't expect anything less." I gestured for her to step away from Tom who was typing furiously on his phone, so thankfully, he didn't notice. "But I don't think this is the right venue."

"Absolutely not," Quinn said, and I thought that was the first time we'd ever agreed on something. "This place is certainly not up to our standards. We need to keep looking. Who thought this was a good idea?"

"Emma. She sent a list of a few places."

Quinn scoffed. "I should have known. She never did have the best taste. Well, I'll find a few new places for us to check out. I already have a list of possible venues. Ryan thought they were great."

Suppress the eye roll, suppress the eye roll. "Great, and I'll find a few, too. We can compile our lists."

Quinn forced a smile. "Great. Well, I have to run. I have a very important hair appointment. See you later?"

Something told me that for Quinn, every hair appointment was "very important." And Quinn was off with another flip of that "very important" hair before I could respond. Apparently I had to let Tom down myself.

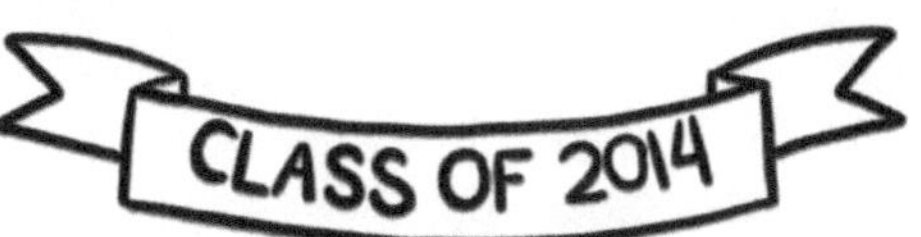

FUTURE ME PREDICTIONS

In Ten Years...

I will be a(n) ___history professor.___

I will live in ___Boston, MA.___

I will marry ___a successful businessman.___

I will have ___two kids.___

I will live in a(n) ___townhouse.___

I will have ___my Ph.D.___

4

That night, I poured myself a chai tea latte, rubbed a clay mask on my face, put on some moisturizing fuzzy socks, and pulled out my old high school yearbooks. I started with freshman year and made my way through all four years of cringy high school photos. I didn't appear in many candid pictures, and all of my formal school photos looked the same. Honestly, I thought I still looked the same. I still regularly got mistaken for a high schooler at work. The number of times I'd had to pull out my faculty ID badge to prove I wasn't a trouble-making student impersonating a teacher was ridiculous.

But I think it was more than my young features that made me feel like I still looked the same. I felt like I still *was* the same. Nothing about my life felt any different. I still lived in this same small town, I still drove to River Glen Academy every day, and I still hadn't done any of the things I'd said I would. It might have seemed silly now, but I had imagined myself more successful at this point in my life. I'd pictured approaching thirty years old with the security of knowing that my degrees were finished, that I'd found the right person, that things were going according to plan. Now I was twenty-eight, and I hadn't even finished my Master's, I wasn't married with kids—heck, I didn't even have a boyfriend—and everything felt unstable and not right.

My phone buzzed, so I grabbed it and saw a text from Eli.

Do you still like cookies and cream ice cream?

Is that even a question? I asked.

No typing bubble popped up, but my doorbell rang, so I headed over to answer. I ordered things off of Amazon pretty regularly, so I kind of just assumed that that was what it was even though they didn't always ring my doorbell. Amazon was pretty much the only visitor I ever got. When I opened the door and saw Eli holding two Coldstone containers, I realized that I shouldn't have been as surprised as I was.

Eli snorted when he saw me. "Nice look," he said, and I remembered the muddy clay all over my face and my hair knotted behind a dingy gray headband that used to be white.

"Shut up," I said. "You're the one who showed up unannounced. How do you even know where I live?"

"I asked Paige," Eli said with a wide smile.

"Oh, I see, so she's just handing out my address without telling me?"

Eli's smile faltered. "Are you busy?"

I gestured to my whole bedtime ensemble. "Do I look busy?"

"No, I just mean do you not want me to— do you still want the ice cream?"

I grabbed a container from his hand. "That's a stupid question."

Eli followed me inside, and I was suddenly very self-conscious not of my face or my hair but my kitchen. I hadn't cleaned up my pile of mail in weeks, and there were some bananas hanging that were probably past their prime. I grabbed two spoons, handed one to Eli, and tried to see if he was looking around my kitchen and silently judging me. I wasn't sure if it was better or worse when I realized he'd been staring at my leggings.

"Are those little Santas on your pants?" he asked.

"So what if they are?"

"April, it's September."

"It's practically October."

"That doesn't make it any better."

"Christmas cheer doesn't have a time limit, you know."

"If you say so."

"Just eat your ice cream and shut up."

Eli happily—and maybe spitefully—shoved a massive spoonful of mint chocolate chip in his mouth and plopped down on my couch. It felt weird to sit right next to him when there was plenty of couch space, but was it weirder to sit far away from him like I was avoiding him? I chose to sit on the same couch but with a cushion in between us.

Eli had always been one of the people I was most comfortable around. He and I had practically lived at each other's houses growing up. We were inseparable in high school. It used to drive Paige crazy, and some of our classmates speculated that we secretly liked each other or something, but we were always just the best of friends. But somewhere along the line, we lost touch, and I hated that. We were super close until we weren't. I know they say it's rare to stay friends with your high school friends and that you drift apart, but this didn't feel like drifting. It felt like suddenly we weren't friends anymore.

And now Eli was sitting on my couch eating ice cream like we'd done a thousand times and teasing me like nothing ever happened and no time had passed. I liked it; I liked knowing that we could be the way we used to be.

Eli pointed at my coffee table with his spoon. "Looking through yearbooks? Is planning the reunion making you nostalgic?"

"Yeah, a little, I guess. Oh my goodness, you'll never guess who I saw today at the Marriott."

"Who?"

"Quinn Pendleton."

"Ew, gross. Why was she there?"

"She wants to help plan the reunion."

"Why? Since when is she Miss Helpful?"

"Since she thinks that I'll ruin the reunion. She obviously doesn't trust me to plan the five-star event she's expecting."

"Does she think you're going to host it in the airport or something?"

I snorted. The local airport was absolutely tiny, but they did host events. It was always a running joke in high school that if a class didn't raise enough funds for a good prom location that they'd get stuck with the airport. No class ever wanted to be the class that had the airport prom.

"Of course not. I'd obviously have it in someone's basement. I have standards, thank you very much."

"Obviously. I mean, a woman who wears Christmas pants in September has the highest of standards."

I reached out my foot to kick him in the side, but he grabbed my ankle instead, forcing me to slide down the couch in a fit of laughter. His hand slid down to my sock, and he recoiled in horror.

"Why are your socks slimy?"

"They're moisturizing socks. They're infused with lotion."

"That's disgusting."

"That's why my feet are prettier than yours."

"Hey, you don't know what my feet look like. Maybe I have the most beautiful feet you've ever seen."

"Not if you think moisturizing socks are gross."

"I think slimy socks are gross, yes, and I don't think that's unusual."

"Ugh, so uncivilized."

He laughed. This was the Eli I remembered. This was how we always were. We could always poke fun at each other without worrying about hurting or embarrassing each other. Eli was always comfortable to be around.

"Okay, so where are you on memory lane?"

"Junior year," I said. "I've been going through them in order."

"Wow, I always swore I wouldn't judge the fashion we wore in high school, but man, what was I doing wearing a puka shell necklace?"

"You were totally into the Hollister look back then."

He scoffed. "As if you weren't."

"Definitely not. I was American Eagle all the way."

"Of course. You were preppy."

"And you were surfer."

"At least neither of us was skater."

I laughed. "A victory for us both."

We ate ice cream in silence for a few moments, and I started to wonder if I should suggest turning on the TV to end the silence, but somehow, the silence didn't really bother me. With most people, I probably would have babbled incoherently to fill the void, but Eli had never made me uncomfortable.

Still, I seemed unsure of what to say. Thankfully, Eli spoke before I did. "So, I didn't actually come over just to eat ice cream and touch your slimy feet."

"Socks, not feet."

"Whatever. I have some venue ideas that Quinn may or may not approve of."

"Really? Like what?"

"I was thinking about the park downtown. It's super pretty with all the lights strung everywhere, and I know they host events. I bet they'd cut us a deal."

"That would be really pretty, and the weather might actually be nice." In Florida, October was an unpredictable month. It could either be gorgeous or excruciatingly hot, and there was no telling until the day of.

"The only downside is we'd have to hire our own caterer for food."

"That's not an insurmountable hurdle. Paige has some connections."

"The other idea I had was the brewery downtown."

"Swan Co.?" I asked.

"Mm-hmm," he answered in between bites of ice cream. "Have you ever been there?"

"No."

"It's in that old warehouse, so it's actually a pretty big space. Since our class wasn't massive, I think we'd fit. And they have good drinks, but they also have appetizer-like food."

"Wow, I didn't even think of Swan Co. Wait, how did you even know about it? It just opened last year."

Eli hadn't been back to town much since he had graduated college. He'd gone to NYU for undergrad and for dentistry school. I didn't even know where he had done his residency. But he hadn't really been back to Florida since he had started dentistry school. At least not that I knew of. If he had come to town to see his parents, he definitely hadn't looked me up.

"I do my research, Corwin."

I couldn't help but smile. In high school, he'd call me Corwin because he knew it irked me. It had actually never irked me when he did it, but I had played along with the gag. Even now, I scrunched my nose at him.

"Besides," he continued, "someone has to bring some class to this event. Clearly Quinn doesn't think you're up to it."

"And you think craft beer is going to change her mind?"

He laughed, and I was reminded of how much I loved the sound of his laugh, that carefree but deep, resonant laugh. It still sounded exactly the same. "Look, I don't really care what Quinn thinks, but I think the rest of the class would be interested in those ideas."

"I'll look into them." I stopped, aware that he was resting an arm on the top of my knee. I hadn't really noticed that my feet were still in his lap from the sock incident. Now that I was aware, I couldn't stop noticing it, acutely attuned to the warmth of his arm on my leg. "Uh, thanks so much for helping. I didn't really want to plan this thing, but I kind of got roped into it. I'm just worried that everyone will think it's totally lame."

"No one's going to think that," he said. "Except for maybe Quinn."

I chuckled. "Plus, I'm way too busy to be doing this, but I just couldn't say no when my boss asked."

"I always hear that teaching is pretty demanding. I guess that's true?"

"It's not even teaching," I said. "I'm doing okay there. I've taught the same classes for a couple of years, so I know what I'm doing. It's just grading that takes a while."

He set his ice cream down on the coffee table and shifted a little, folding his arms across each other on my knee. Again, I was aware of the warmth. "Then what is it?"

I sighed. If I couldn't talk to Eli, then who could I talk to? "I'm in grad school right now, and—"

"Wait, you're in grad school? Why didn't you tell me sooner? That's awesome! I know you always wanted to go."

"Well, I'm just going part-time, taking night classes and all that. Some online."

"Who cares? You're still doing it. History, I assume?"

I nodded. "Master's. I'm almost done. I'm working on my thesis right now. I've just kind of hit a wall."

"What do you mean?"

"When I did my proposal defense, my committee and I decided to change a pretty significant part of my plan. I think it was for the better, but now I'm overwhelmed trying to play catch-up with research and writing."

"How long is the whole thesis supposed to be?"

"Minimum of fifty pages."

"And you have?"

"Thirty-five."

"That doesn't sound so bad. It's only fifteen pages. You're a great writer."

I snorted again. "You haven't seen any of my writing since the twelfth grade when I was writing about *Hamlet*."

"That's not true. You asked me to proofread that one paper freshman year of college."

I burst out laughing. I had taken what was supposed to be a basic chemistry class to fulfill my science requirement, but it had turned out to be some kind of class for pre-med majors. I had been drowning in coursework, and our final assignment had been to write an 8-10 page paper. I didn't even remember what I had written about because it hadn't made sense. I'd sent it to Eli for help. He was always better at science than me. I guessed dentistry shouldn't have been a shock.

"That hardly counts," I said.

"Fair. But still, fifteen pages is manageable."

"Sure, if you're not working full-time grading papers and trying to plan a reunion you weren't even sure you were going to attend."

"Why wouldn't you attend?"

"Why would I?"

Eli furrowed his eyebrows, and I could tell he genuinely didn't know the answer to the question he was asking.

"The only reason to go to a reunion is to show off how much more successful you are than everyone you knew in high school. It's a chance to prove that you're doing well, better than anyone thought. It's kind of like a metaphorical middle finger to the high school haters."

He smirked. "The high school haters."

"Yes. The high school haters," I said with a perfectly straight face before I let myself laugh a little bit. "I don't know, I just thought I'd be more successful than I am now."

Eli started stroking my knee ever so slightly with his thumb. "What makes you say you're not successful?"

"This just isn't what I had planned for my life. I had a lot of goals that I don't feel like I've accomplished."

"That doesn't make you a failure, you know. Sometimes life just works out differently than you imagined. I thought I was going to be a professional soccer player, remember?"

I did. Eli had been the star of the soccer team. He'd had multiple college offers, but a torn ACL junior year had ended his chances. He'd had surgery and tried to recover and rehab it as much as possible, but he just hadn't been able to get back to the level he'd been playing on until it was too late. I remembered watching him practice drills after soccer season had ended, frustrated with how well he was doing when it was too late.

"A severe injury is not the same as just not accomplishing something."

He absent-mindedly traced the outline of Santa's face on my knee. "Maybe not, but I probably never would have pursued NYU, and I never would have thought about dentistry."

"How did you end up at dentistry?"

He wagged a finger. "Uh-uh, no distracting from yourself. My point is that you're exactly where you're supposed to be in life. Getting a Master's at twenty-eight does not make you a failure by any stretch of the imagination."

"If you say so."

"I do say so," he said, jutting his chin out in mock confidence. "And I'm never wrong."

"Pffh, yeah, okay."

"I just think that you shouldn't put such harsh deadlines on yourself and your goals. You're still accomplishing them. Who cares if it isn't when you thought it would be?"

I threw my arms out to the side. "Uh, everyone we went to high school with."

"I promise no one from our class is sitting around wondering if you already have a Master's degree or not."

"I guess."

"Can I ask something though?" he said with a softer tone, and he avoided eye contact. "What made you wait if you wanted to do it sooner?"

I hadn't waited. I had gotten delayed. There was a big difference. "Life just happened. I decided it was better to start working and get back to it later. I just didn't think it would take so long."

Eli seemed like he wanted to say something else, but he seemed to decide against it, instead staring at his own thumb which was still methodically running back and forth across my knee. It felt nice. I found myself hoping he wouldn't stop.

As if aware of my thoughts, Eli stopped suddenly. "Well, I should probably get going. It's late, and it is a school night, Ms. Corwin."

"Gross, do not call me that," I said, laughing. "Are you doing anything this weekend?"

He froze. "Why do you ask?"

"I was thinking maybe we could swing by the park and the brewery and see what they have to say."

He started nodding suddenly, almost too emphatically. "Oh, right, of course. Yeah, I can do that. Saturday morning?"

Odd. "Yeah, that'd be perfect."

"Do you want me to pick you up here?"

"No, that's okay. We can just meet there."

Eli avoided eye contact again. "Okay, great. I'll call them and see when they want us to come, and I'll text you a time."

"Sounds great."

Eli got up, packed up his ice cream, but hesitated before walking toward the door. "I don't know if I said it already, but it really is good to see you again, April."

"It's good to see you too, Eli."

"I—I've missed you."

"I've missed you, too," I said, but I wanted to say more. Why had we stopped talking? How did such good friends lose touch and never try to repair it until now? Why had it taken our class reunion to get back in touch?

And what could I do to make sure we never lost touch again?

But I didn't say anything. I watched him walk out the front door and missed the way it felt to sit next to him, feet in his lap, his arm on my knee. I missed the sound of his voice and the light in his eyes when he smiled. Most of all, I missed the way it used to feel to be with Eli. Spending time with him again reminded me why I missed him. It made me think that I had to protect our friendship this time, to make sure we stayed close just like we had always been. Eli's friendship was too important to lose.

River Glen Academy
Faculty Job Application

Applicant: April Corwin

What do you think is the most important habit or belief you could communicate to your students?

I believe that all students should develop a lifelong love of learning, particularly about the past and what we can learn from it. Too many people view school or education in general as something they have to do, a stepping stone to their actual futures, but education is so much more than that. In any profession, it's so important for people to possess a spirit of learning. This enables people to continue to be successful in their chosen careers and fields. History in particular is so applicable in so many parts of life. We can learn so much from past civilizations and cultures, and it is so critical that we never stop learning from them. I hope that my students will see the value in history and that they will continue to pursue learning, whatever form that may take, long after they leave the classroom setting.

5

— · —

Project days in my classroom were always days of loosely organized chaos. I had assigned a project about Reconstruction to my AP U.S. History class, and they'd been working on it for a few days. This was one of my favorite projects that I assigned because I felt like the kids really got a lot out of it—more than they would get from listening to me drone on about it—but after all the work on posters, it always looked like a tornado blew through my classroom.

"Ms. Corwin?" Ellie asked. "I have a question for you."

I walked toward her group's table. Teachers probably weren't supposed to have favorites, but Ellie had to be pretty far up the list. She was such a hard worker, and she was the kind of student who actually enjoyed school. She reminded me of myself in some ways: a very driven, intrinsically motivated girl. I didn't know if history was her favorite subject or not, but if it wasn't, she certainly displayed enough enthusiasm to fool me.

"What is it?" I asked.

"Since we're doing our project about Lincoln's assassination, should we talk about how his plan for Reconstruction was likely different from Johnson's, or is that not relevant?"

"That's a great idea, Ellie," I said. "Lincoln's assassination is significant not just because the president was murdered, but it happened at a really crucial time in the country's history. We have no way to know exactly what he would have done and whether it would have been better than what Johnson did. It would be a really cool element to include."

"Okay, perfect. I wanted to talk about it, but I didn't want to go off-topic. Thank you!"

And with that, she went right back to sketching her design for the poster.

Students like Ellie made me actually like teaching high school. She always went above and beyond what I required simply because she got excited about learning. I wished more students were like her.

My first year as a teacher, I had this one totally wild class that made me question everything. Now that I was in my sixth year teaching, I could confidently look back and say that that class was by far my worst in my career—unfortunately, it happened to be right at the beginning. I totally questioned everything about myself as a teacher that year because everything just seemed hard. It was a pretty big class, mostly boys, and it had seemed that they were competing to win the title of Class Clown. None of them had taken my class or me seriously. Granted, I was twenty-two straight out of college teaching students only four years younger than me, but still. Classes like this and students like Ellie made it all worth it.

My watch buzzed, and I saw the first words of an email from Ryan. I felt my cheeks get hot. I did a quick scan of the room and saw that all of the students seemed to be working diligently, so I slipped over to my desk to check the email.

Hey, Corwin!

I couldn't help but cringe. Ryan and I were not best friends in high school like Eli and I were, so he didn't know how much I hated that.

He probably thought I didn't care because everyone did it, including Eli, but Eli did it jokingly. I was sure Ryan thought it was endearing.

I heard from Quinn Pendleton, and she said neither of you were thrilled by the Marriott. I trust your collective judgment. Let's pass! Quinn sent me a list of ideas, but I'm sure you have some ideas, too, and I'd love to hear them. Do you mind sending me a list when you get a chance? I'm happy to do what research I can from a distance if it helps.

I shouldn't have been surprised that Quinn had already slipped an email in ahead of me without even mentioning that we discussed working together on this.

I also have some ideas for events or activities I'd like to run past you. Would you mind sending me your phone number? I think it would be easier to talk over the phone or video chat or something. Looking forward to hearing from you!

I had to remind myself that I wasn't in high school anymore and I shouldn't get all excited that Ryan Bennings was asking for my phone number. Of course he was asking for it. We were working together. It only made sense. But still, the flutter in my chest was distracting.

Hey Ryan!

That sounded casual, right? Should I put another exclamation point? No, that would be so weird. Maybe I shouldn't put one at all. *Hey Ryan.* Oh, absolutely not, that was so stiff, and it sounded like I was mad at him. One exclamation point.

I do have some other location ideas. I'm at work right now, but I'll send you a list later today. I would also love to hear your ideas for activities—I don't have any idea what to do! Feel free to text me so we can set up a time to talk. Looking forward to it!

After deleting and retyping that last exclamation point several times, I added my phone number and clicked send. Okay, that sounded good, right? Friendly, but not overly needy? Basically, if I could avoid sounding like Quinn, I would feel that I succeeded.

I took another lap around the classroom to check on posters. Some were closer to being complete than others, but overall, I was happy with the progress. Aside from minor distractions that were just the norm when teaching high schoolers, everyone had been working really well.

This was probably the only thing that I felt was working really well in my life right now. I was good at teaching. I wouldn't have said that a few years ago, but now that I was six years in, I felt like I'd hit my stride with it. I was good at lesson planning, I was good at building rapport with students, and my AP pass rates were among the highest in the school. This wasn't the job I wanted or thought I would have, but I was at least glad that I was good at it. In the middle of the chaos of planning this reunion and dreading its arrival and trying to figure out how to repair my relationship with Eli and finishing my thesis and generally feeling like a failure in my personal life, I was at least doing well professionally, and that was some kind of small consolation.

My watch buzzed again, and I saw that this time it was a text from Ryan.

Ryan: *Hey! So glad you replied. Any chance you're free to talk tonight?*

I slipped my phone out of my back pocket and replied.

Me: *Sure! What time were you thinking?*

Ryan: *I get off work at six, so how about six-thirty?*

Ryan: *As long as you don't mind me eating dinner on camera while we talk.*

Ryan: *If you do mind, we'll have to wait until seven.*

Me: *Six-thirty is fine. Feel free to eat.*

Ryan: *You're the best :)*

It felt kind of weird talking to Ryan like this. I used to dream of talking so casually with Ryan that we could joke like this and use emojis. Ten years later, it was finally happening.

It occurred to me after the fact that he asked about eating on camera. Which meant we were video chatting later. I had known that was an option, but we hadn't even discussed it. He had just assumed. Or maybe that was what he wanted? Either way, now I had to look cute tonight.

I opened my phone camera and checked my appearance. I hadn't washed my hair in three days. That was *not* good. I'd have to run through the shower really fast tonight before we talked. Somehow, I felt that greasy hair would definitely show on camera.

"Ms. Corwin?" Connor said from the back of the room. "Where should we put our posters if we're not done yet?"

I snapped out of my ridiculous musings and checked the clock. The bell was about to ring. "Uh, you can stack them on top of the bookshelf in the back."

"And we can work on them tomorrow?"

"Yes, and Friday. Remember that they're due first thing Monday."

"Okay," Connor said, and the bell rang. "Thanks, Ms. Corwin!"

"You're welcome. Have a great day, everyone!"

As the students trickled out of the classroom, I started shuffling papers and tried to make my room look somewhat presentable for my next class. My thoughts drifted while I worked. Maybe Paige was right. Maybe working with Ryan was meant to be. Maybe I shouldn't fight it.

***

I had considered curling my hair earlier, but I was pressed for time, so instead, I decided to blow dry with a round brush to at least give it some volume and body. I'd let my hair go longer in between highlight appointments lately because I'd been so busy, but I only had the slightest golden highlights in my dark brown hair, so I was hoping it wouldn't be obvious on camera. I made a mental note to make an appointment before the reunion.

I sat down on the couch and checked behind me to see what my backdrop would be. Did other people do that? Check what would be behind them in a video call? Or was I just weird and obsessive? My kitchen was behind me, and it was relatively clean thanks to Eli showing up unannounced last night, resulting in a panic cleaning session late last night when I should have been sleeping.

I adjusted my hair at least ten times and waited for him to call. Or was I supposed to call first? I seriously debated calling him, but thankfully, my phone started ringing before I could, so I answered.

It took a moment for the call to connect fully, but when it did, Ryan seemed to be still adjusting his phone to get the right angle, and I found myself noticing the wall behind him. It was a beautiful old brick wall, and it looked like it was his kitchen, too, with a rack of pots and pans hanging high above some wooden floating shelves. It was a gorgeous rustic kitchen.

"Corwin! Can you hear me?" he asked, and he was louder than I thought he realized, so I notched the volume down a bit.

"I can hear you."

He was just as handsome as I remembered him being—maybe more so since he was older and looked more mature. His blonde hair that used to be long and shaggy was cut medium length now, pin straight as always. He was clean shaven, and he still smiled the same way: a little goofy, very charming. He was wearing a light blue button down shirt with the sleeves rolled up, and it looked so business casual that it was somewhat unexpected. I still pictured him in either his football jersey or a polo shirt.

"Awesome," he said.

"Where are you?"

"My dining room. Well, sort of." He picked up the phone and spun it around so I could see his whole kitchen. "I kind of just shoved a table here against the back of the couch in the living room and called it a dining room."

He was right: there really wasn't space for a table, but he'd crammed one in. Even though it was cluttered with furniture, it was a beautiful room. He had a pretty modern kitchen with stainless steel appliances and black cabinets, but against that brick wall, it looked really nice.

"You're up in Boston, right?" I asked.

"I am."

"How is it?"

"It's really great. I've been living here since college. I got a really good job with an accounting firm up here. I just started renting this townhouse about a year ago, though."

"It looks really nice."

"Yeah, it is. I didn't really want to rent anymore, but I couldn't pass this place up, and I got a raise, so it was actually in budget."

"I'm so jealous. I love Boston. I'd kill to live in a townhouse in Boston."

"Oh yeah, didn't you go to school up here?"

I had to stop myself from visibly bristling. No, I had not gone to Boston University as I had planned. Just one more thing that I had failed to do.

"No, I ended up going to Florida State."

"Nice, how was that?"

I shrugged. "It was good. I liked it. So, you're an accountant now?"

He nodded. "Yeah, crazy right?" It was crazy. I never would have pictured him doing a career so serious—so *boring*. "But I love it. And the firm's been really good to me."

Ryan was practically living my ideal life. He was in Boston with a good job, living the dream. He was exactly the kind of man I had imagined myself marrying in high school. In many ways, he still was.

"So you're a teacher at River Glen, huh?" he continued. "That's wild! How do you like it?"

"I like it," I said, and at least I felt honest about that. "It's busy but cool."

"Yeah, when the office contacted me and told me that someone in our class was on the faculty, I didn't realize it was going to be you. I'm glad it was though."

My ears perked up. "Yeah? Why is that?"

"Look, I love the people we graduated with, but not everyone would take this seriously. A lot probably don't care. But I know you'll do everything you can to put together an awesome reunion."

"Thanks, Ryan. That means a lot."

"Of course. I mean it." He smiled, and I smiled, too, and it felt easy to talk to him. We had always been friendly in high school, but we had never hung out much outside of school events. In high school, friend groups and cliques meant so much, and it just felt impossible to cross those lines. Now, none of that mattered.

"You know," Ryan said with just a hint of hesitation, "when I get to town, maybe we can get together."

"Get together?"

"Outside of the reunion planning, I mean. Maybe we can go to dinner or something? I'd love to catch up more once we're in person and not staring at each other through screens."

Was Ryan asking me out? Or was this totally normal, and I was just reading too much into it?

"Sure," I said. "I'd love to."

He smiled. "Great. I'm really looking forward to it, then."

"Me, too," I said, but I couldn't believe what was happening. Ryan Bennings just asked me on a date? And I accepted? Oh, Paige would never let me live this down.

"So," he continued, "let me tell you about some of the ideas I have for the reunion."

"Let's hear it," I said.

Visual Voicemail

April? This is Mom. I guess you're in class, but I need you to call me back as soon as you get this. It's your dad. He was in a car accident. I'm on my way to the hospital to see him. The doctors are saying he'll be okay, but he got hit pretty hard. Some idiot ran a red light. Please call me back, honey. I—I don't know what to do.

6

— • —

"Mom, Dad," I called out as I walked through their front door. I tried to stop by a couple of times a week to check in on them. "Are you here?"

"In the kitchen, honey," Mom called out, so I rounded the corner to the kitchen.

They had downsized a few years ago, and it was still hard to picture this house as their home. I still remembered every detail of my childhood home. It didn't help that it was just a few streets down, so I had to drive by and see it all the time. I was devastated when they sold the house, but I understood: after my dad's car accident, he hadn't been able to go back to work the way that he had been, so they had needed to downsize to a one-story house with a smaller mortgage payment. Still, it was hard to see this as "home." But maybe that was also just part of growing up and moving out.

The one thing that didn't change was the smells of my mom's cooking emanating from the kitchen. She was making stew, and it smelled spectacular, warm and hearty. I set my bag down on the kitchen counter of the peninsula and pulled up a bar stool.

"How are you, honey?" Mom said.

"Good."

She stopped stirring the pot on the stove top and eyed me suspiciously. "What's going on?"

"What do you mean?"

"Well, I ask you that question every day, but it doesn't normally make you smile. Usually you sound tired or annoyed."

"Gee, thanks."

"You know what I mean. Good news?"

"Well, you know how I told you that Mr. Quentin roped me into planning the reunion?"

"Yes."

"Well, I've got some help now. Ryan Bennings called me last night."

"Who is Ryan Bennings? Do I know him?"

"Mom," I said, exasperated. "You remember Ryan. He played on the football team. We were lab partners in chemistry."

She snapped her fingers. "Oh, that's right. Didn't you use to have a crush on him?"

"Mom!"

"What? Am I wrong?"

I slammed my face into my hands. "Oh my gosh, I'm not still in high school. We're just working together."

"But you're happy about it?" Her voice lilted like a question, but she seemed to say it as a statement.

"I'm happy to have help, yes. I don't have time to plan a reunion."

"And you're happy that that help is coming from Ryan What's-his-name?"

"Bennings, and yes. He's always been a nice guy."

"Mm-hmm," she mumbled without looking up, just stirring her stew with a smirk.

"Oh, stop it. It's not like that. Eli is helping, too."

"Eli Forrester?"

"Do I know any other Elis?"

"His mom told me he was back in town. I didn't know you had caught up with him."

"Yeah, I ran into him at Paige's shop the other day."

She stopped stirring suddenly and looked up over her glasses at me. "His mom said you two hung out last night?"

I was not surprised that Mrs. Forrester would tell my mom something like that if she knew. Our moms had been best friends since we were little kids. I pretty much assumed that anything one of them knew, the other also knew.

What I did not expect was that Eli told his mom about last night. He crashed my house at night with ice cream and then told his mom?

"We weren't really hanging out," I said. "He just came over, and—"

"He came over? To your apartment?"

"Mom, it's not like that. He just wanted to catch up. We haven't talked in so long."

"Yes, why is that? You two used to be so close."

"Honestly, I don't know. He got kind of distant when we were in college. I don't really know what happened."

"Well, that's in the past now. I'm glad you two reconnected. So you're working with Ryan and with Eli?"

"Ryan is in Boston. We just video chatted last night to go over some ideas. That's all."

"Does Eli know?"

"Why does that matter?"

Well," she said wistfully, avoiding eye contact, "you know he always had a crush on you."

"Oh my gosh, he did not."

"He did. You just never wanted to acknowledge it."

"Okay, maybe when we were, like, eight, but that's it."

"That's what you've told yourself for years, dear, but it simply isn't true. He always liked you."

"Then why didn't you say something sooner?"

"I did, but you were a teenager. You usually ran away screaming and plugging your ears."

I folded my arms. "That does not sound like me."

"The fact is that he always liked you, but you never saw it or felt it, I suppose. Maybe he thinks he's got a second chance now."

"Mom, he lives in New York. Besides, that was a million years ago. We're adults now."

"If you say so. So how was your chat with Ryan?" she said smugly.

"I see what you're insinuating, but you're still wrong."

"Wrong about what?" my dad said as he walked in from the garage holding too many grocery bags.

I jumped up and took some bags from him, despite him trying to swat me away. "You shouldn't try to do this in one trip. You could've come in to ask one of us to help."

"I don't need help carrying groceries. Besides, what's the fun in making multiple trips?"

"Less wrist pain," I said, setting the bags on the counter and starting to unpack them.

My dad wasn't frail, and I probably worried about him more than I should have, but the accident had taken its toll. He had pretty chronic back pain, and sometimes his knees would give out on him. His chronic back pain had meant that he had cut back on his hours after I graduated and brought in less income. Hence the downsizing.

"So what is your mother wrong about?"

"That Eli Forrester has always liked her," she said.

"Oh," he said. "I didn't realize that was up for debate."

"See?" she said with a grin.

In high school, a lot of people had joked that Eli and I were like a couple, and that included my parents, but it had always been just that: a joke. I hadn't really thought that any of them were serious. Now we were twenty-eight, and my parents *still* thought Eli liked me?

"All I'm saying is that I'm glad to have help from Ryan and Eli with the reunion, and it was nice to see Eli again and nice to connect with Ryan again. That's it."

"If you say so, honey," my mom said, returning to her cooking and my dad to his unpacking, but somehow I knew this wouldn't be the last I heard of it.

March 25, 2014
Re: Financial Aid Status Decision

Thank you for your interest in Boston University, and congratulations on your acceptance to the undergraduate class of 2018. We appreciate your enthusiasm for our institution. We recognize that attending college is a significant investment which can weigh heavily on many students. Unfortunately, however, we are unable to offer you financial assistance for the 2014-2015 school year.

Please note that this is not a reflection of your ability as a student nor is it a dismissal of the unique challenges you may face attending college. We have many students who apply for aid each year, and we are unable to offer aid to everyone. Our financial aid is very competitive, and we have many high-achieving students in need. Based on your family income and other data supplied to us via the FAFSA, we are not in a position to offer you any scholarships or grants.

Should anything change with regard to your financial status, please send us appropriate documentation as soon as possible for us to review.

We apologize that we could not give you better news. We wish you all the best as you graduate high school and pursue higher education.

Sincerely,
Boston University Financial Aid Office

7

—·—

I parked my car outside of Eli's parents' house and texted him that I was there. It was kind of weird sitting outside of Eli's house like this. We used to do this all the time in high school—pick each other up at each other's houses. But as soon as I was in his parents' driveway, it felt totally normal. His parents' house still looked the same as it always did. The only thing that looked different was I thought they had painted the shutters brown, and it looked like his mom had planted a few more flower bushes. She loved to garden. I hoped their new house would still have space for a garden so that she could keep it going.

Eli came out carrying a cardboard box, so I rolled down my window.

"You know we're not setting up for the reunion today, right?"

He rolled his eyes. "Very funny."

"What's with the box?"

"It's a box of my stuff from high school. Apparently my parents decided it has to leave their house right now. Can I stash it in your backseat? I'll take it with me later."

Eli shoved the box into the backseat and got in the passenger side. I pulled out and headed toward the park downtown.

"Take it where? Aren't you staying with them?"

"Well, yes."

"What are you going to do, stash a bunch of boxes in your rental car?"

"Actually, I'm moving."

"Moving?" I asked, but it took a moment for me to register what Eli was saying. "Wait, you're moving back to River Glen?"

"Yes," he said while looking out his window.

"Like, to help out your parents for a while?"

"Well, that, but—I don't know. I might stay. I'm renting an apartment downtown. Month-to-month lease."

"Why?" I said, but I immediately regretted the way I said it. It sounded accusatory, maybe critical. I hadn't meant it that way, but I struggled to imagine why anyone would willingly move back here. Eli was one of the lucky ones who had gotten out of this small town. Why would he choose to come back? Sometimes River Glen felt like a black hole that was inescapable, always sucking everyone back in.

He looked at me with a bit of shock, and I found myself glad that I was driving so I had an excuse to avoid eye contact. "Why not?" he said. "I don't exactly have ties anywhere else."

"What about New York?"

He shrugged. "Just college friends. It's not the same as River Glen." He pointed to his right. "Oh, parking spot."

Good parking spots downtown were hard to come by, and though I hated parallel parking, I hated parking in the garages more, so I headed straight for the spot Eli spotted. It took me more tries than I'd like to admit to get my car in, and Eli mocked me the whole time.

I wondered what he meant that New York wasn't the same as River Glen. Wasn't that the point? Eli had always been so excited to go to NYU. It was all he talked about in high school. At first, it had seemed like a pipe dream—a River Glen Academy student getting into NYU—but Eli had worked hard to make it a reality. We'd daydream about living in New York and Boston and visiting each other in our respective cities. It had sounded like the perfect plan, and when we both got accepted, it seemed like it was going to be a reality. That was until Boston fell through for me.

I never really told Eli what happened or why I didn't go to Boston. My grandfather had died earlier that year, and he knew that had been rough on me. We were really close. Senior year had been one hit after another. My dad had inherited my grandfather's estate and sold it, but right after, he had lost his job, and we'd lived off of the money from that sale for months. Eli knew all of that.

What he didn't know—what I didn't tell anyone except Paige—is that Boston University had calculated my financial need based on my dad's full-time job and the substantial estate inheritance, neither of which we had by the time Boston University actually processed everything. We'd tried to explain everything, but it was too late. The government forms had been submitted, and according to those forms, I had more than enough money to go to school out-of-state.

That was the real reason I had chosen FSU. It wasn't that I had decided I liked FSU better or that I wanted to stay in Florida close to home or that my dad went there—all of the reasons I had told people when they asked—but that I had needed in-state tuition and an alumni family discount. I'd been too embarrassed to admit that to anyone, especially Eli. I had wanted him to go to NYU without feeling bad that I wasn't going to Boston. He had never pressed me for details, and so I had let it go.

As we approached the park in the center, Eli said, "See? The lights are really pretty, and I think we would have enough space out here. We could set up tables, maybe put the food spreads over here, and a dessert table right there."

I raised an eyebrow. "Dessert table? Are we doing dessert?"

"We are now." He folded his arms. "I can't believe you even thought about doing this without dessert. That's absurd."

I laughed. "Clearly."

"Thoughts on a dance floor?"

I couldn't help but laugh again. "Who's going to dance at a high school reunion?"

"You never know." He shrugged. "It could be fun."

"We'd have to hire a DJ. I'm not sure that's in the budget."

Who needs a DJ for dancing?"

"Uh, everyone?"

"April, I'm disappointed in you. Where's your spontaneity?"

Before I could answer, he took my hand and started dancing me around the big tree in the center of the park. I couldn't stop laughing at how ridiculous we must have looked dancing without any music playing. Eli slipped a hand to my back, and I was hyper aware of how he pulled me closer to him and started humming some song I couldn't place in the moment. My laughter faded when I noticed how he maintained eye contact with me, his dark blue eyes glowing when the sunlight peeked through the tree branches and hit his face. I never used to feel this way when Eli and I hung out, and I was having a hard time identifying the feeling. It was the same feeling I'd noticed the other night when he had been touching my leg. It was not a foreign feeling—just foreign to being with Eli.

He spun me out and bowed dramatically, so I laughed and curtsied. A thought flashed through my mind that I hoped that none of my students were around to see that—I would never hear the end of it.

"So, he said, slightly winded from his performance, "dance floor?"

I rolled my eyes and smiled. "Sure, why not? I guess if no one dances, we can still listen to music."

"Perfect. So dance floor right here, right?"

Eli went back to mapping out tables and displays with his armspan, but I wasn't totally paying attention. It had always felt like there was a weird schism between us once I had decided to go to FSU. I used to wonder if he had found out the real reason and resented me for not telling him. Or maybe he was mad that I didn't move up north with him. I wasn't sure, but I was glad that he was acting more like himself now.

"So what do you think?" Eli asked, and I snapped out of it.

"I think it's perfect. Although I'm not sure Quinn is going to agree."

"Quinn Pendleton?"

I nodded. "She offered to help. She met me at the Marriott the other day, and let's just say she was not happy about the choice. You should have seen her face when I said that Emma Wilson is the one who suggested it."

Eli laughed. "Yeah, those two never got along."

Emma Wilson had been one of those rare girls in high school who was really popular but still really nice. She had been in the "it" crowd, on the cheerleading squad, and always had a date to homecoming or prom, but she was genuinely a kind person, and that had made everyone love her all the more. Quinn had always kind of resented her. Technically, Emma had been way more popular than Quinn, and that was always a threat to any queen bee. I remembered in middle school they had been best friends, but something about that switch from eighth to ninth grade totally changed everything in friend groups. In fact, Paige and Eli were the only people I had stayed good friends with in that transition. Everyone else had become a friendly acquaintance, someone I would study with or talk to at a party but not someone I would see during the summers in college or whom I texted regularly now.

"So, are you going to check with her before we book it?" Eli asked.

I twisted my mouth and shook my head again. "Nah. I'm the one Mr. Quentin asked to do this. Besides, I'm sure Ryan will love the idea. I'll send a picture to him right now."

I snapped a picture of the park and texted it to Ryan, but I felt Eli fidgeting next to me.

"What's up?" I asked.

"Nothing."

"You sure?"

Eli nodded, but I felt that weird distance again, the distance that had ended our friendship and that had only reared its ugly head one other time since he'd gotten back to town. Why did my bringing up Ryan elicit that reaction? In high school, it had always annoyed him that I had a crush on Ryan, but we were seventeen. Did he really still care about Ryan? Weren't we past that?

"Do you still want to see the brewery?" he asked.

I shrugged. "Do you think there's a point? I really like the park idea." As if on cue, my phone buzzed, and I saw that it was Ryan sending a thumbs up to my park picture. "Ryan agrees. Let's just book it. It'll be prettier than the brewery anyway since that's an old warehouse."

"Sounds great."

It was so hard to reconcile the Eli I'd always known, the one who joked with me and was always there for me, with the one who shut down on me regularly. Weren't we dancing in the park shamelessly just moments ago? I couldn't ignore the way Eli was avoiding eye contact with me now, but I couldn't forget the way his eyes looked while we were dancing, and I could still feel warmth on my back where his hand had been.

***

Eli and I had managed to coordinate a catering tasting right at lunch time, so we were totally getting a free lunch. I mean, I guess it wasn't technically free because the school was going to foot the catering bill for the reunion, but hey, that was a cost the school would incur, not me. A teacher's salary meant taking the free food wherever you could get it.

Paige had put us in touch with an independent catering company that she knew of. They had catered small events all over town and were trying to expand. A high school reunion for a small school was exactly the kind of thing that would help them expand without biting off more than they could chew.

We'd agreed to meet them at the Donutisserie because Paige was willing to let us take over a corner of the shop for a tasting. They had brought samples of their most popular buffet-style dishes for us to try. We hadn't really gotten into them yet, but they smelled wonderful.

"Okay," Karen said as she opened the first tray. Karen made most of the food since she'd gone to culinary school. Her business partner Jeannette handled the technical details. "The first thing I brought is a crowd pleaser. Not to brag, but I make the best alfredo pasta you'll ever have."

Eli and I both laughed, but when I tasted it, I had to admit that she was right: it was incredible.

Karen continued, "This one is always popular, and we can add chicken or steak or some other protein if you want it."

"It's delicious," I said. "But do you think it might be too messy for the park?"

Eli nodded. "I was thinking the same thing."

"We could always make it with a different pasta," Karen said. "So instead of fettuccine, we could do rigatoni penne or something that's easier to eat."

"Well, I think that's a contender for sure," I said.

Karen rolled back the foil on her next container. "Option number two is a surf and turf kind of thing. We could serve a meat and a fish of your choice. Clients typically want steak and shrimp or lobster or sometimes pork and salmon. We can do pretty much any side dish you would want."

"As much as I love seafood," I said, "that would probably be outside of River Glen Academy's budget. It smells delicious though."

Karen gestured toward the plate. "I totally understand. Please have some anyway. No sense letting it go to waste."

Eli snagged a shrimp skewer. "Don't have to tell me twice."

Karen said, "I do have one other option. Hang on, let me get it from the back."

Eli polished off the shrimp and looked up at me. "Are you sure we can't afford this? Because it's delicious."

I laughed. "Yeah, pretty sure. The alfredo's great though."

"For sure. My parents want to have a housewarming party once they officially move. I think I'll suggest that they get this catered so that my mom doesn't make herself crazy trying to make too much food."

"That's a great idea. So, have they found a house yet?"

"I think so. They found one on Magnolia that they really like. My dad was kind of nitpicking some really little things about it, but I think Mom'll talk him into it."

"What was he nitpicking?"

"Oh, you know, the usual. The front door is an ugly color, the backyard fence needs to be repaired, the flower boxes need to be rebuilt because Mom hates them."

"Those are all super fixable problems."

He spread his arms. "That's what I said, but you know how he is. Everything always has to be perfect."

"So are you going to offer to paint the front door for them so that they put in an offer?"

He laughed. "Already did. Mom's picking out paint colors. I offered to help Dad with the fence and flower beds, too. Between the two of us, I figure it won't take very long. Plus I've got the time. You know, when you don't have me running around to catering appointments."

I laughed, by my mind drifted to what Eli had said the other day. He was seriously considering moving back to River Glen. That seemed so odd to me. He couldn't wait to get to New York. I couldn't imagine what would make him want to come back here.

"Hey, can I ask you something?" I said. "About what you said the other day?"

"Sure."

"Are you really thinking of moving back to River Glen?"

He nodded slowly. "Yeah."

"Seriously?"

"Seriously." After a while, he added, "Why, is that surprising?"

"I mean, kind of. I thought once you moved to New York that you'd never come back."

He shrugged. "Yeah, I mean, I guess I kind of thought that, too. I don't know, I guess it's different when it's actually a reality."

"What do you mean?"

"New York was great and all, and I loved NYU, but I just don't see myself there long-term. It doesn't feel right."

"Couldn't handle driving in New York City, could you?"

I'd always used to tease Eli in high school that he would hate driving in New York. He was such a nervous driver back then, and he always panicked whenever anyone honked at him or got mad at him in traffic. I'd told him that if he couldn't handle River Glen traffic, then he would never be able to drive in New York and would have to take the subway everywhere, another thing he was afraid of. I wondered now if that had changed. Had he been riding the subway for the last six years? Did he have a New York driver's license?

He laughed, too. "I could handle it just fine, thank you. But no, New York is just so impersonal. It's so cool, don't get me wrong, but I kind of felt like a drop in the ocean there. I missed the community of River Glen."

"You mean everyone having their noses in your business all the time?"

Another laugh. "Honestly, yeah. Nobody cares about me in New York. I was just another person walking down crowded streets. Here, I don't know. It's just different. I like knowing that I'm surrounded by people who care what happens to me."

"I guess that makes sense," I said, though I wasn't sure I meant it. Honestly, I could have used a little anonymity in recent years. It was hard teaching alongside people who were your teachers and remembered every weird thing you did in high school. It was hard having your parents' friends ask how you were doing and if you were dating anyone. It was hard getting asked "Have you finished that Master's yet?" pretty much all of the time.

"I don't know," Eli continued. "Maybe I'm turning into an old man, but I want to raise a family, you know? I want to get married and have kids. I want to coach little league soccer and build flower pots for my mom and get to know people. I just don't feel like I can do that in New York. Too many people, you know? Maybe that sounds silly—"

"It doesn't sound silly."

"I just think about my childhood—our childhood," he added, pointing back and forth between me and him, "and I just loved growing up here. When I picture raising kids, I picture River Glen. I can't help it."

"Yep," I said, "you're definitely turning into an old man."

He scoffed. "Yeah, I set myself up for that one."

"Seriously though, I get it. I liked growing up here, too. It is a great place for a family."

And I meant that. I'd been a happy kid growing up here, and I could see his logic. Still, I couldn't help feeling like River Glen wasn't the only place that kind of life was possible. There were suburbs all over the country. It didn't have to be River Glen. He felt nostalgic because he'd left River Glen, and now he missed it, but as someone who pretty much never left, it was easy to feel trapped here. I wanted a family and kids, too, but I didn't think I wanted them here. I wanted to be anywhere else.

But sitting here looking at the way Eli smiled when he talked about his ideal future, it was hard to ignore the fluttery feeling I had. What was it about being around Eli again that caused that feeling? I told myself that it was because he was talking about having a family—and when is it not attractive to hear a man in his late twenties with a serious career talk about wanting to raise kids?—but it was also just Eli. Eli was somehow the same as he'd always been and yet different, more mature somehow. He still looked and sounded the same as he always had, but I felt like the way I saw him was what had changed.

Before either of us could say anything more, Karen returned with another tray, and this one was divided into segments.

She said, "This is my wild card offer. We could do a Tex-Mex buffet, kind of a create-your-own-taco kind of thing. This is a little more casual, but maybe it would make more sense at the park?"

Eli and I each eagerly made a taco and ate, marveling at how delicious they were.

"Yes," I said, "This is perfect. I think this is the winner."

"I agree," Eli said.

"Do you think Quinn will hate the idea?"

"Oh, absolutely," Eli said. "Just makes the idea even better."

"Fantastic," Karen said, then unwrapped another platter exposing several miniaturized desserts including cheesecake, shortcake, mousse or pudding, and pie. "I know you didn't mention desserts, but I took the liberty of bringing some samples anyway. I can make them all individual servings like this, so people can just grab what they like. I figured that everyone likes dessert, right?"

"Told you," Eli said, flashing me a smug smile.

"Fine, yes to desserts," I said, and Eli pumped a fist, shouting, "Yes."

"Oh, I have an idea," Eli said. "What if we have her cater the pre-game dinner, too? We could do the alfredo."

"That's a great idea."

We had been told that there would be a dinner served before the football game, but no one had given me any details on who was supposed to plan that. I assumed that Mr. Quentin was assuming I would tackle that, so he probably wouldn't even notice that bill when it crossed his desk.

"Fantastic," Karen said, clasping her hands. "I'll grab Jeannette and have her bring over the contract, and we can hash out all the details. Please, eat those desserts so that I don't take them home and eat them myself."

"Say no more," Eli said, and we both grabbed a mini dessert.

APRIL CORWIN
STUDENT

OBJECTIVE

Soon-to-be high school graduate with honors seeking admissions to Boston University.

EXTRACURRICULAR ACTIVITIES

- **Class Secretary (11th-12th Grade)**
  - maintained notes during student government meetings
- **RGA Tribune (9th-12th Grade)**
  - editor-in-chief of the school newspaper responsible for editing all copy and assisting in assigning stories to other staff members
  - writer of feature articles
  - work on layout
- **Congressional Classroom (11th-12th Grade)**
  - studied with local senators in Tallahassee
- **Varsity Volleyball (10th-12th Grade**
  - assistant captain (12th Grade)

WORK EXPERIENCE

2012-2014

Publix

- Bagger and cashier
- customer service

EDUCATION

2010-present
RIVER GLEN ACADEMY

- 4.26 GPA
- honor roll all four years
- AP Classes: AP Language, AP Literature, AP Modern World History, AP U.S. History, AP Government, AP Pre-Calculus, AP Chemistry, AP Seminar

VOLUNTEER WORK

Childcare Worker - River Glen Baptist Church (2011-2014)

- takes care of two-year-olds during Sunday school hour
- cleans toys and surfaces

Volleyball Summer Camp (2011-2014)

- teaches elementary students how to play volleyball in a two-week summer camp

Tutor - River Glen Academy Elementary (2010-2014)

- tutors elementary students in reading, math, and study skills

8

When I had agreed to sponsor the Model United Nations club at school, I honestly had no idea what I was in for. I'd thought that it would be the kind of thing that students did just to put it on their resumes for college applications; I hadn't thought they would take it so seriously. I didn't have a huge group—small private school problems and all—so we often had to double people up on multiple teams. At first, I had worried that maybe that would be too much pressure and workload for the students, but they loved that they got to do multiple things.

I was starting out the school year with almost an entirely new team. Last year's team had a lot of seniors, so most of the club participants had graduated. I had two current seniors who were acting as team leaders, but mostly, I was training the younger students. Though I preferred teaching the upperclassmen, I did enjoy that in Model UN, I had all grades in high school. It gave me a chance to work with some of the students before I had them in class. There were few things more exciting than a Model UN student being excited to have me as a teacher after knowing me for a few years.

Because it was still early in the school year, we weren't really at the debate and negotiate stage of things, so this week's meeting was mostly about how to research. Sometimes I felt wildly inadequate to be coaching the Model UN—I only ended up with it because the teacher I replaced had coached it, and no one else wanted it—but this was a part I knew very well. Historical research had always been something I loved. It was why I had wanted to major in history and get an advanced degree in history. Someday, after I was done with my Master's and not feeling so burned out on research and writing, I knew that I wanted to go for a PhD in history. When I thought about how much work that would be, I really questioned my sanity, but the idea of being "Dr. Corwin" was too appealing to pass up.

"Ms. Corwin?" Dennis said as he came up to my desk with his laptop. "I'm having trouble finding anything when I search on JSTOR. Everything that comes up is super random and not at all related."

I smiled and slid his laptop toward me. JSTOR was the database we used for the students to research, but it was a bit finicky sometimes, and the students struggled with it. Apparently the shining jewel in my graduate school crown was gaining the ability to teach high schoolers how to use research databases. "Sometimes you have to play with the search terms a little bit. So, instead of searching for just 'human rights,' try adding 'Middle East' to your search terms."

"Oh, okay."

"And you might want to narrow down the time frame. There is so much research that exists about human rights in the Middle East, and a lot of it is dated too far back to be relevant for you. Try looking at just the last twenty years or so. If that's too narrow, expand it to fifty, but you really don't need the super old stuff for your part of the project."

Dennis clicked on a source about human rights violations in Afghanistan. "So this one would work, right? It's not super old, and it seems related."

"Yes, that one is probably fine. Make sure you skim it to check before you add it to your list of sources."

"Okay, thanks!"

Dennis went back to his seat and clicked away diligently. I had been a little surprised when Dennis joined Model UN. I didn't really think he liked history all that much. He was an average student in class, and it hadn't seemed like he had an extracurricular involvement at all except during football season. Lately, though, he'd been pouring everything he had into researching his part of the project. I had the group planning a conference about human rights violations and how involved the UN should be in handling them. I had one group representing an alliance of countries with claims that sovereignty was being violated and another group representing an alliance of countries introducing legislation to prosecute UN members who violated the existing human rights statutes. I was going to have them debate each other before we went to the local conference to debate another school. I didn't have a ton of students, so I accepted anyone who joined, but Dennis had really surprised me lately. He was so serious about his research and was determined not to let his group down. It didn't always come easily to him, but he was persistent, and he welcomed any direction that came from his team leader Bennett. I was impressed by his work ethic, and I had hoped that his team would welcome him. So far, it seemed that they had.

Sponsoring extracurriculars gave that unique perspective that just didn't come from teaching in a classroom. The students were a bit more casual at club meetings than they were in my class, and I liked getting to see another side of them. This was also where I learned a lot about what the students wanted to do in college and beyond. While I had some students in Model UN who were interested in pursuing a career in politics, I had others who joined it for a variety of reasons. Some wanted the public speaking experience because they wanted to be lawyers or something like that, others joined because they weren't necessarily very athletic, but they were very smart and loved to research, some joined to be in an activity with friends, and others, sure, joined for the resume boost, but was that such a bad thing? They still did the work and learned some skills along the way. I really didn't mind that. Other teachers got really annoyed by students who joined activities for that reason, but I never did. I had a bit of a reputation as a "chill" teacher for that reason. I just never understood that philosophy as a teacher. Why did teachers expect teenage students to act like adults? Of course they picked things for fun or avoided things that weren't. That was normal. The teachers I remembered loving as a student never got frustrated with teenagers for acting like, well, teenagers, and as a result, we usually worked harder for those teachers because it felt like they were on our side. As a teacher, I wanted to be the same thing. I promised myself that I would not get frustrated with teenagers for being teenagers—instead, I would find ways to make history matter to teenagers. Did it always work? Absolutely not, but when it did, it felt so good.

I glanced up at the clock and saw that our meeting was almost over. "Five minute warning," I said. "Find a good stopping place and send your team leader the research you found. Next week, we're going to start organizing everything and pulling points you can use in your debates."

The students started shuffling, and the conversation shifted from human rights to homecoming dresses in record time. I laughed out loud when I heard the discussion.

"Homecoming is still a month away," I said.

"That's basically no time," Katie said with a hair flip. "You have to get a dress way earlier than that."

I laughed again. Katie was such a funny student to have in class. She was so smart but also hilarious. "Somehow, I think you'll find the right dress. I believe in your ability to find the perfect dress."

"Well, I *have* to. It's senior year, you know? It has to be perfect."

"I'm sure it will be," I said while still typing away on my laptop. I was trying to knock out a few pages of my thesis during the club meeting. I had finally gotten a narrative together, and it felt like it was finally working.

"Are you going to homecoming, Ms. Corwin?" Katie asked.

"I'm not sure."

Katie and some of the other girls gasped. "Ms. Corwin, you *have* to go. You're the coolest teacher."

I smiled. "I'm glad you think so, but my high school reunion is that weekend, so I don't know if I'll have time."

"I heard you were planning the reunion. Just plan it so you can do both!"

I chuckled. "If only it were that simple."

Another student, Anna, hopped up on a desk. "Is it weird that you're going to your high school reunion? Like, does it feel like you've been out of high school for ten years?"

I shook my head and gestured around the room. "Not at all. Mostly because I'm still here."

"I don't think I could ever teach at River Glen," Anna said. "It would be too weird."

Katie folded her arms. "Oh, I would do it. Then I could be Ms. Corwin's coworker."

"Ew," Anna said with a laugh, "but then you'd have to call her April. That just sounds weird." She turned to me. "Do you call your old teachers by their first names?"

"No." I laughed hard. "I cannot bring myself to do it."

Katie said, "Well, I think it would be cool to be a teacher here. But not history. Something more exciting like science. No offense, Ms. Corwin."

I smiled. "None taken."

Everyone else trickled out, but Katie and Anna stayed behind. "Did you always know you wanted to be a teacher?" Anna asked.

"Sort of. I thought I would be a history professor."

"Like at a college?"

I nodded. "But I ended up here instead."

"Would you ever quit and go to a college?"

"I don't know," I said without really thinking about it, but once the words were out, I was surprised by them. I was even more surprised to find that that was the honest answer. I wanted to answer them honestly, so I simply said, "I like teaching high school."

"Why?" Anna said, letting her surprise creep into her words. Most high schoolers were surprised that anyone liked teaching high school. So many dislike high school when they're in it, so it's difficult to imagine high school as a positive. I hadn't disliked high school, but I certainly hadn't loved it. I was just kind of in the middle.

"Because of stuff like this," I said, and it was true. I liked high school because I liked the age and the atmosphere. I liked coaching Model UN, I liked helping students apply to college, I liked going to football games and musicals. College was sometimes impersonal. I could recall no more than six or seven professors I'd had that I thought were meaningful and more than just someone at the front of the room talking. In high school, every teacher, for better or worse, had an impact. "I like getting to do this kind of stuff with you guys."

"Wow, Ms. Corwin," Anna said. "That must be why you're such a good teacher. I could never teach high schoolers. We're so annoying."

Katie laughed and elbowed Anna. "Anna, you're not supposed to say stuff like that to our teacher."

Anna pointed at me. "I'm not telling her anything she doesn't already know. Be honest, Ms. Corwin, we're annoying, right?"

I laughed. "No, you're not. High schoolers are way more fun to teach than anyone else."

"If you say so. Bye, Mrs. Corwin!"

The girls left, and I tapped out the last of the paragraph I was on in my own thesis. I remembered thinking I would hate this job because of exactly what Anna had said. Weren't high schoolers annoying? Wouldn't I get irritated? Wouldn't I want to quit?

But I didn't find them annoying or irritating, and I didn't really want to quit. Maybe I wouldn't stay in River Glen forever, but teaching high school hadn't been nearly as bad as I had thought.

***

After the Model UN meeting, I drove to Publix, picked up some cookies and fried chicken, and headed straight for my parents' house. We'd made a habit out of having dinner together every Thursday night. When I had first come back to River Glen after college, I'd moved back in with my parents, and I had been so busy at work trying to learn how to be a teacher that I hardly saw them. My mom had insisted that I at least have dinner with them every Thursday so that I would take a break and talk to them. When I moved out, I'd missed them so much that I showed up for dinner the very next Thursday. Now it was an unofficial habit.

I pulled into their driveway and grabbed the Publix bag, eager to eat the chicken that had smelled so good the entire drive there. We almost always had Publix fried chicken on Thursdays because it was the easiest thing to pick up, and it was always delicious.

Mom opened the door before I even reached it, and I walked straight to the kitchen and plopped the bag down on the table in the breakfast nook. My parents had a dining room, but we only used it on Thanksgiving and sometimes at Christmas. The rest of the year, it felt silly for three of us to sit at a table meant for six.

"Where's Dad?" I asked as I pulled out some plates and napkins.

"Finishing something up in the office. He'll be out in a minute."

"He's not working too hard, is he?"

"No, honey, it's just a sales report." My dad did some bookkeeping for some local businesses on the side to make a little extra money. It was so easy for him to do it quickly.

"Well, he better hurry before I eat all of his chicken."

"So how was your day?" she asked.

I shrugged. "Fine. Normal. I had Model UN after school."

"How did it go?"

"Really well, I think. I've got so many kids who are new to it, but I think they're embracing it. Plus I really like the topic this year. They're really getting into the whole human rights thing."

"Seems so heavy."

"It's politics, Mom, of course it's heavy."

Sometimes my mom didn't really get the whole "history teacher" thing. Whenever I talked about politics or the uglier parts of history I was teaching, she'd balk at it. My mom didn't love politics to begin with, and she avoided talking about it at all costs. She found it distasteful, something that people only ever argue about without getting anything done. While that might have been true in some arenas, I had always liked politics. It was more fun to teach. High school students liked to argue, so even if they didn't love history class, they at least got invested if I let them argue.

"And they like looking up human rights violations?"

"If you phrase it like that, it sounds really weird," I said. "But yes, they like the real world application. The UN had a similar human rights convention not that long ago, so they actually feel like they're doing something real with this."

"Well, that makes sense."

"They're actually excited about this one, and that makes my job a lot easier. I'm so excited to see what happens."

"What happens when?" Dad said as he walked in from the office. "You didn't eat my wings, did you?"

I rolled my eyes and shoved the chicken box across the table. "No. I was talking about Model UN."

"I wish my school had had Model UN. That would have been so cool."

My dad, on the other hand, loved politics, always had. He had liked to debate random topics with me for fun when I was in college, much to my mother's chagrin.

"So, how is your thesis going?" Mom asked, deftly changing the topic of conversation, though only slightly. After all, my thesis was fairly political.

"Good, I think. I finally found enough primary sources to analyze. Now it's just weaving it all together."

"Sounds simple enough," she said.

I snorted. "It's not simple. But it feels more possible, I guess."

"I knew you'd figure it out," she said.

I laughed. "I'm glad someone did. I was starting to think I would never figure it out."

"Oh, that's ridiculous. You're so smart, and you've been working toward this for a long time. There was no reason to think that you wouldn't be able to do it."

How did moms do that? How did they always make things sound so simple and easy to understand and tackle? My thesis was so scary for so long, and I was still scared of it despite being the midst of it, but to hear her talk, I would have thought my completing a Master's thesis was the simplest and most natural thing in the world.

"I'll be glad once it's all done," I said. "The thesis, grad school, the reunion, all of it. I'm just so busy right now."

Dad raised an eyebrow. "Not too busy for Scrabble, I hope? Mom and I think today's the day."

I laughed out loud. My family played Scrabble all the time, but I always won. I'd been winning since I was a little kid. It drove my parents nuts that they couldn't beat me, so it had become kind of a joke in our family.

"Yeah, right," I said. "Ready to lose?"

"Not this time," he shouted as he ran off to the office to get the game. Mom and I cleared the table, and he set up the Scrabble game with great efficiency. It was a finely-tuned science at this point. My dad always kept score, my mom always played first, and my dad always complained about having too many vowels. Then, usually, I'd play some really unusual word with high-scoring letters and swamp them before the game even started.

This had probably been the best part of coming back to River Glen after college. I'd been so disappointed that I wasn't going to Boston, and I hadn't been thrilled about teaching high school at the time, but I was glad to spend more time with my parents. At first, it was just because of Dad's accident, and I'd told myself I would move on once he was doing better, but I had never really moved on. But why should I? Why was part of adulthood leaving your parents in the dust? Sure, I wanted to be my own person with a career and a family, but should that prevent me from playing Scrabble and eating fried chicken with my parents? I didn't think so. Some people thought I was too attached, that I was immature or childish for staying so close to them, but personally, I found people who stubbornly ran away from their parents simply because society told them they were supposed to to be far more immature. It was a childish insistence on leaving the past behind and rejecting the family that got you there. Looking at my parents set up a game of Scrabble, I felt sure that would never be me regardless of how old I got.

We each drew our letters, and Dad immediately shouted, "Aw, rats! I got four I's."

"Honey," my mom said as she played the word "steam," "you're not supposed to say what letters you have out loud."

"What difference does it make?" he said, holding his forehead in distress. "She's going to beat us anyway." When I played the word "oxidize" off of Mom's E, my dad threw up his arms. "See? We've lost already."

Do you think Mr. Tucker knows his shirt is untucked in the back?

Do you think he knows that his pink shirt does not match his purple pants?

Test on Friday. Study session later with milkshakes?

It's a date.

9

—·—

"Please do not tell me that you *still* listen to Nickelback."

Eli gasped then turned up the radio in his car to make a point. "How dare you? Nickelback is quality."

"They are not," I said. "They never have been."

"Everyone secretly likes Nickelback," he said. "It's just popular to hate them, so people convince themselves that they do, but they're actually good."

"I'm pretty sure you're making that up."

"I am not," Eli said as he turned the wheel, heading down a familiar street. "Everyone knows all the words to Nickelback songs because they secretly like them."

"Or because they're on the radio literally all the time."

"And why are they on the radio all the time if nobody likes them, huh?"

I put my hands up in surrender. "Fine, I give. You're clearly too stubborn for this conversation."

"I'm not the stubborn one here."

Eli kept driving down Holly Drive, and that was a street I knew really well. This was where Eli's parents had lived, though they were moving now. This was also where my parents used to live. Our house had been four houses down from Eli's, and we had been at each other's houses constantly. We passed the house I grew up in, and I looked out the window at it. It was such a beautiful house, and I loved growing up on this street. Everyone knew each other really well, and I had always felt safe and loved in this neighborhood. It was the kind of street that almost looked unreal, like it was a street from some kind of simulation of a utopia that someone didn't realize they were trapped in, but it was real.

"So is the house you wanted me to see on Holly Drive?" I asked.

"It is."

Eli had called me and asked me to help him look at a house he was considering putting in an offer on. It was still so surprising to me that Eli was seriously considering moving back to River Glen. Even though I only ever knew Eli right here, it had become so easy to picture him in New York, so it was weird to get used to picturing him here. What did Eli look like as an adult in River Glen? I tried to picture a white picket fence, him pushing kids on a swing set in the backyard, maybe a grill on a back deck. It was so idyllic. Were we entering that phase of adulthood when we had idyllic suburban lives and became parents? It felt more like high school was yesterday rather than the reality which was that we were pushing thirty.

He pulled into his parents' driveway, shifted the car into park, and smiled at me.

"Did you need to pick something up?" I asked.

He shook his head. "This is it."

"Wait, what? Your parents' house?"

He nodded. "I was thinking, what better family house than my own? I always loved the house, so why not?"

"So are your parents not going to sell it then? Just give it to you?"

"No, I would still buy it from them. I want them to get the money from the sale for their new house, but yeah, maybe this is the one."

I looked up at the house. It was a craftsman style house that was painted a sage green and had a gabled roof with cedar shake. Eli's mom's gardening in the front so beautifully complemented the green paint, and I knew that his dad pressure-washed the brick columns on a regular basis, so they were spotless. It was one story, but I knew that it was much deeper than it looked; Eli's bedroom was in the very back of the house. I'd always loved the craftsman style, but I appreciated it more looking at it now. Eli was right: it was the kind of house you raised a family in.

"Do you want to see it?"

I laughed. "I've seen it, Eli."

"I know, but not as my prospective adult house. Besides, my parents have moved out a lot of their furniture, so it's mostly a blank canvas. I have some ideas for some renovations I want to make, but I want another opinion." He rubbed the back of his neck with one hand and snapped a couple of times with the other. "Well, I want your opinion."

Why did it make my heart flutter that he wanted my opinion specifically about his house? "Well, all right then. Let's go."

We walked up the sidewalk, Eli unlocked the door, and I was surprised by how different the house looked without his parents' furniture. The house had never been huge, but now it looked endless with sprawling rooms that seemed capable of holding much more furniture than I knew it could hold. The front was the living room, and it stretched back into a dining room and a small den in the back. The kitchen, which wasn't visible from the front door, was tucked to the side of the dining room. Unless his parents had done some renovating recently, I knew that the kitchen hadn't really been updated since the '90s, so it would definitely need some work, but the main living spaces were still beautiful.

Eli flicked on the lights, and they reflected off the bare hardwood floor. "So obviously the floors are in great shape because my dad waxed them constantly, and they already patched some of the little holes from the stuff my mom had on the walls." He pointed to the patches that were white against the beige paint. "I would definitely paint, and I want to do some work on these built-in bookshelves because they're a little rough, but I think this room is perfect."

I looked over at Eli who was staring at his childhood living room with his hands on his hips and a smile on his face. It was nice seeing him so excited about something. He lit up, and I understood why he felt this was the right house.

He ushered me into the kitchen, and I saw that I was right: it needed to be renovated. "So obviously I would have to redo this kitchen completely, but I think I'm okay with that. It's a chance to make it my own, you know? I'm thinking white oak cabinets and a white stone countertop. Plus, I think I can knock out this weird half wall thing and do an island instead. But I'm not taking out that wall. I like the floor plan of this house."

"You've really put a lot of thought into this."

He nodded, still smiling. "I think it feels right. I still have some appointments to see some other places, but it's hard to walk away from this."

"I get it. It was hard to get over it when my parents sold their house and downsized."

Eli hopped up on the kitchen counter and rested his forearms on his legs. "It's a weird phase of life, isn't it? Like we're adults, but it still feels like we're kids."

"Oh totally. Sometimes it feels totally unreal that I'm the adult in the room at school. It's weird to be responsible for kids."

"Did I ever tell you that I think it's so cool that you became a teacher?" he asked, and I shook my head. "You're made to be a teacher. I would have loved to have had a teacher like you."

I laughed. "No you wouldn't have. I am way too chill for you."

"Oh, you think I'm not chill?"

"No, you never were. You were such a nerd in high school."

He gasped. "I was not."

"You were! You were that kid that told the teacher when she forgot to collect the homework."

"Because I always did it! I wanted credit."

I pointed a finger at him and squinted. "See? Nerd."

"Oh my gosh, whatever." He rolled his eyes and grabbed my hand that was pointing a finger at him, but my breath hitched when he did.

"You can't tell me that you weren't a total nerd. Still are."

"Oh, am I?" he said, pulling my hand so that I moved closer to him. I brushed against his knee and couldn't help but glance down at it for whatever reason. I looked up into his eyes that were looking down at me, mischief sparkling in his face. I became aware that at some point he had put his other hand on my upper arm. Every point of contact that existed between the two of us felt electric and warm.

It was becoming increasingly hard to ignore the way I was starting to feel around Eli. At first, I had brushed it off as just a side effect of seeing him again after so long, but here we were making jokes and teasing each other like we always used to do, but he never used to hold my hand or touch my arm when we were teenagers—at least not like this, in a prolonged way with more affectionate contact than a playful slap on the arm required.

But there I was standing in Eli's old house that might become his new house, the house he would bring a wife home to and raise kids in, and I was starting to think that I wanted to be a part of that. The way he was sitting on the kitchen counter now felt so natural, and I had visions of him sitting like this while I cooked at that stove, while kids did homework at the dining room table the way we used to do. Was that totally crazy? Probably. I was actually fantasizing about marrying my childhood best friend, and that just seemed totally insane. But was it? If I was just letting my thoughts and feelings run away with me, then why was he holding my hand and looking at me like that? Was I really imagining the spark I felt every time he touched me? Was I really alone in feeling like I never wanted him to let go?

"So," I said after clearing my throat awkwardly, "have you found the one?"

He raised his eyebrows. "The one?"

I gestured around me with my arm, but he didn't remove his hand. "This. The house. Is this the right house?"

He cleared his throat and looked away. "Oh, right. I'm not sure. I want to see some other options to make sure I'm not letting myself get carried away by sentimentality."

Was that what I was doing? Was I getting carried away by sentimentality? Eli and his family and his house had always meant so much to me. Was I getting swept away by the nostalgia? A thought drifted through my head that maybe this was what happened when you had a high school reunion—everyone got sappy and nostalgic and wanted to reminisce. But Eli still hadn't let go of my hand, and I still didn't want him to.

"So," Eli said, and he finally did let go of my hand but didn't take the hand off my arm. "What do you think about having dinner tomorrow? We could hash out some reunion details and make sure we've got everything nailed down."

"Sure."

He dropped his hand, and I hated that I felt obligated to step back. He smiled and hopped off the kitchen counter. "I'll pick you up around six if that works for you."

"Oh, we can meet there if that's easier."

Eli furrowed his eyebrows. "There's no point to that. I'm going to drive past your apartment complex to get to the center of town. Six?"

I nodded. "Six."

I followed Eli out of the house, and I was certain that something had discernibly shifted between us, and I was also starting to think that that wasn't such a bad thing.

***

On Monday, I wandered the campus during my free period. Sometimes, I just needed to stretch my legs and get some fresh air instead of sitting at staring at my computer. Was I behind on grading and probably should have spent the time catching up? Sure. But some days the most beneficial thing I could do for my productivity was to take a break.

I took the long way to the other building to check my mailbox, passing the main office, and while normally I would have just kept on walking, I saw someone waving to me through the tinted office glass window. The door swung open, and I was surprised to see none other than Garrett Dunny, one of the first students I ever taught.

"Ms. Corwin!" he said as he threw his arms out for a hug. Garrett was a senior when I taught him, and he'd always been significantly taller than me at six feet, but somehow now he seemed even taller, though I suspected it was an illusion. A lot of teenage boys were so skinny like their height had resulted from their entire body being stretched out. Now that he was a little older, he didn't have that kind of gangly look anymore, and I was surprised to see that he was relatively dressed up in a polo and dress pants. He always used to complain about the dress code at RGA.

"Garrett, good to see you," I said. "How is it going?"

"It's good," he said with a bright smile. "I'm in a paramedic training program now."

"Really? That's fantastic. You were a biology major, right?"

"Yeah. The paramedic program isn't too long, so hopefully I'll finish soon."

"That's so exciting."

Garrett Dunny was the last student I would have expected to become something like a paramedic. He was such a class clown in high school that he had earned the nickname "Funny Dunny" from his classmates. I didn't think he took anything seriously, but apparently I was wrong.

"I dropped by to bring my little brother lunch for his birthday, but I wanted to stop by and say hi to some of my favorite teachers, too."

"I'm one of your favorite teachers?" I asked, and I tried not to sound too incredulous.

"Of course," he said, and I could tell that he was serious because I was so used to seeing him not serious. "I didn't think I was capable of much back then, but you never let me settle, and I needed that. I'm glad you didn't give up on me."

"You've always been smart, Garrett. You just needed to harness it."

He nodded. "I know. I'm glad you knew that then. I'm sorry I was such an idiot in class. I must have driven you crazy the way I was always bouncing off the walls."

I laughed, mostly because it was true, but it was funny how much more self-aware people became after high school. "You were never an idiot."

"Eh, I don't know. Anyway, thanks for putting up with me."

"I'm so happy to hear that you're doing well. Thanks so much for stopping by."

"Sure thing. Bye, Ms. Corwin!" he said with a wave as he walked toward the cafeteria.

I headed to the workroom to check my mailbox and ran into Elaine. Elaine was probably my favorite coworker. She was a little older than me, so she had kind of taken on a mentorship role with me, but she was also still young enough to be relatable.

"Hey," she said, glancing up from her stack of papers. "What's up?"

"I just saw Garrett Dunny."

She set her pen down and looked at me with surprise. "Really? He's here?"

I nodded. "He brought Jimmy lunch, but he stopped to tell me that he's glad I didn't give up on him. He's training to be a paramedic."

"You know, that makes a lot of sense—the paramedic thing."

"It does? He seemed like such a goofball."

She laughed. "Yes, those goofballs often turn out really well. Garrett was always a sweet kid. He just had too much energy and didn't know what to do with it. A really hands-on career makes a lot of sense."

"I guess so."

"So he thanked you?"

"Yeah, that came out of nowhere. I had him my first year. Do you remember that crazy seventh period class I had?"

"Oh, yes, that was quite the initiation to teaching that you had."

"Oh my goodness, I don't know how I survived that one."

"I remember hearing that class talk about you. They liked you. They were kind of wild, but they knew you cared."

"Wow, I do not remember it that way at all."

"You never do in the moment. Teaching is such a weird career because you're so critical of yourself all the time. Every day is like a performance, and it's really vulnerable. Most teachers—the good ones anyway—always think they're not doing enough, but the students see everything the teacher is doing."

"I guess so. I remember just getting so frustrated with him all the time. I must have written him at least four or five detentions by the end of the year."

"But see? He remembers that you didn't give up on him. You could have ignored him, but he needed consequences."

I nodded slowly. "I don't know, I guess I've always just kind of felt like I'm not a natural at teaching. I feel fairly confident in myself now, but those first few years were rough."

She laughed loudly. "Everyone's first few years teaching are rough. None of us ever really know what we're doing, and it's easy to look back on those years and wonder why someone ever hired us."

I snorted. "That's for sure."

"But I never thought that about you."

"Really?"

She nodded. "I've mentored a couple of others, but you stand out. You care, and that's the best that students can get from teachers is to know that they care. Garrett got that from you, and look at him now. He's turned himself into someone really great, and while you may feel like you didn't have anything to do with that, he thinks you did, and that's what matters."

I found myself getting teary listening to Elaine talk because that was at the root of my problems as a teacher. I often didn't feel like I was good enough. I used to wonder how I would ever become a college professor if I couldn't handle being a high school teacher, but that was totally the wrong thinking. What mattered was how students perceived me, and even one of my most difficult students ever felt valued by me. And, in fact, I *could* handle being a high school teacher. I was a pretty decent one.

Elaine got up, straightened her pile of papers, and gave me a pat on the back. "You're doing great, April."

And for the first time in a while, I actually believed it.

Hello
test Friday!
Shakespeare test in English class
• Shakespeare was born in Stratford-upon-Avon
• His wife's name was Anne Hathaway ← Weird
• Wrote 37 plays
• Wrote over 150 poems
• Plays performed at the Globe Theater
Three categories of plays
tragedies
comedies
histories
OIC DY
THE HUNGER GAMES
April + Eli = BFFL
FOREVER!
and ever
Need to study:
★ Hamlet
★ Macbeth
★ Julius Caesar
★ finish reading Othello

10

Sitting at my usual table at the Donutisserie, I took a sip of my latte and rubbed the side of my head, trying to shake the fatigue that was increasingly distracting me from my thesis. I had to finish at least this section so that I would feel good about making some progress. After that, I only had one more section to go, and that last section wasn't even the hardest, but I knew that after that would come notes from my supervisor, and I was honestly pretty scared of getting those. He was such a stoic, unreadable person, and I really had no idea if he thought I was doing all right or if he thought that I was a totally incompetent idiot. It really was a toss-up.

I only had a couple of pages left to write, and normally I could write a few pages like it was nothing, but the scale of this research and this claim was just so vast. Finding primary sources of Southern Union sympathizers was a bear alone, but proving that they were credible and stringing a narrative that connected them all was much worse. I had settled on the notion that divisive politics caused people to hide their true beliefs rather than to engage in meaningful conversation or debate and had used the Civil War example as proof that this has been a problem for all of America's history—a problem that is unique to a free-thinking democracy—but the more I wrote, the more I felt like I was just making stuff up.

"How's it going?" Paige said as she plopped down into the chair across from me. It was pretty slow right now, and she had just finished a rack of pumpkin spice donuts: the first of the season.

"Terrible."

"Actually terrible, or what you think is terrible?"

I scrunched my nose. "I don't like what you're insinuating there."

"You're always convinced that everything you write is terrible, and it pretty much never is. Hasn't your supervisor signed off on every-thing so far?"

"Sure, but that doesn't mean anything."

"Why not?"

"Maybe I've totally conned him into thinking that I know what I'm doing, and he has no idea that I'm a total fake."

Paige shrugged. "Well, if you're smart enough to con your professor who has a PhD from Berkeley, then you're smart enough to write the paper."

I shoved my computer away from me. "Stop using logic against my impostor syndrome!"

"Never," she said in a deep, throaty voice that made me laugh. "Okay, for real though, you need to take a break. Do something fun tonight. Do you want to go see a movie with me or something?"

"I can't," I said, not looking up from my computer that I had pulled back and was trying to desperately to extricate words from my brain to put on the screen. "I'm having dinner with Eli."

"Excuse me?"

I looked up. "What?"

"You're having dinner with Eli, and you're just now telling me?"

"What does it matter?"

"Because you're having *dinner* with *Eli*."

"Oh my goodness, it's not like that. Eli and I are friends. We always have been."

"Sure, but it's different now."

"Why?"

"Because we're adults," Paige said as if I were supposed to understand the significance of that statement. "You're not just hanging out with a childhood friend."

"Except I *am* hanging out with a childhood friend."

"But that childhood friend is an adult now with a successful career who somewhere along the line got super good-looking."

I flicked my eyes back to my computer. "Eli was always good-looking."

Paige waved her hand in front of my computer screen to force me to look at her. "What?"

"Oh my gosh, don't make it weird. Like you said, we're adults. I can't acknowledge that a man is attractive without you making it a whole thing?"

"Any other man, sure. But Eli? Girl, you're going on a date with Eli tonight."

"I am not," I said with a scoff.

"Okay, fine. How did this dinner thing get planned?"

"He asked me yesterday."

"*He* asked *you* to dinner?"

I rolled my eyes. "To finalize details for the reunion."

"That was just his excuse to ask you out."

"It was not."

"Then why didn't you guys just finalize reunion details right then? Why ask to meet at another time over a meal?"

"Because we were at his parents' house. He wanted my opinion on whether or not he should buy it."

Paige waved her hands dramatically, and her hair fell into her face, but she made no effort to move it. "Wait, wait, wait. Eli is *moving* back to River Glen?"

"Maybe."

"So you're telling me that Eli Forrester is moving back to River Glen, buying his childhood home, and asked you on a date?"

"Two of those things are a maybe, and he did not ask me on a date."

"Okay, I know you've always been resistant to the whole concept that Eli likes you and always has—"

"He does not."

"—but he obviously wants to date you."

I sighed. "It's about the reunion. He's helping me plan until Ryan gets to town."

"Ooh, yeah, what about Ryan?"

"What about him?"

"What if Ryan shows up and asks you on a date? Can you really go on a date with Eli when you've been hoping Ryan will ask you out when you get to town?"

"Okay, you are getting way ahead of yourself here. Ryan isn't even here, and he might ask me out or he might not. And Eli is not asking me out either."

She rolled her eyes. "Is it so inconceivable that men would want to ask you out?"

"It's a little inconceivable that two men from high school would want to ask me out suddenly at the same time."

"Look, you can convince yourself that I'm wrong all you want, but the fact is that Eli has always liked you. He liked you in high school. Why do you think he used to get so mad at you when you would drone on about Ryan?"

"Because I was an annoying high school girl?"

She shook her head emphatically. "It's because he liked you, and he was desperately hoping that you would finally notice."

"If that's really what happened, then why didn't I notice?"

"Because he was such a big nerd!" Paige shouted way too loudly, drawing the attention of the other customers in the shop.

I shushed her. "That's exactly what I said."

She raised an eyebrow. "So you were flirting with him, huh?"

I went back to typing and avoided eye contact. "Whatever. You're distracting me from writing."

"Fine." She held her hands up in surrender. "But when you're at dinner with Eli tonight, just think about what I said."

I waved a hand at her until she walked away, and I was annoyed at her intrusion, but I couldn't shake the idea that maybe she could be right. Hadn't he held my hand? Hadn't he kept a hand on my arm while he talked? Hadn't he stroked my leg the other night? Hadn't he danced me around the park downtown?

Hadn't he asked my opinion on the house he wanted to buy to raise a family?

And hadn't I been unable to ignore the way I felt when his eyes gazed into mine?

Not that I would ever admit any of that to Paige—she'd never shut up about it. I decided that I would be rational, that I would observe Eli with an open mind, no preconceived notions, and no feelings. I would be an objective observer, looking for clues without reading anything into them like Paige had. I would be a historian looking for evidence and documenting my sources.

And I definitely would not get distracted by the glow in his eyes when he smiled.

Dang it.

***

Eli had been kind of vague about where he was taking me for dinner, and I hated when guys did that. How on earth was I supposed to dress if I didn't know where I was going? I had decided to wear a periwinkle blue floral sun dress and a white denim jacket with nude wedges. I decided that looked nice enough without looking like I was trying too hard. I reused my curls from the day before, recurling a couple of pieces to make it look more finished and intentional. That way, if Paige was right and it was a date, then I looked good. And if I was right and it wasn't, then I still looked a little casual. I was still kind of annoyed that I was actually planning my outfit according to whether or not this was a date. Paige and my parents had me psychoanalyzing every single thing Eli did. So when Eli pulled into the parking lot of Alex's A+ Grill, I nearly laughed out loud.

Eli and I had practically lived at Alex's A+ Grill. It was owned by this really sweet older man in town. He was an army vet, and he opened that restaurant in retirement. It had used to just be called Alex's Grill, but when Alex's wife—whose name, oddly, was Alexa—had started working there full-time, she'd insisted that the name include her. Alex thought that change was a clever way to slip her name in. Alexa didn't find it nearly as funny, but they were just the cutest couple. Eli and I used to study here any time we weren't at one of our houses. This was where everyone went to eat after late night games or study sessions.

And it wasn't the kind of place people went on dates. Did that matter? Was that an indicator of how Eli expected this night to go? Or had it been chosen because the place was special to us?

As he put the car in park, Eli said, "How do you feel about some cheeseburgers and nostalgia?"

I laughed. "Perfect."

Alex made the best cheeseburgers, and that was practically a food group in my mind, so I never turned away a chance to eat one.

Eli and I walked into the restaurant, and Alex waved when he saw me, but when he spotted Eli, he smiled and headed over.

"Oh my goodness, is that Eli Forrester?" he said. "As I live and breathe. I haven't seen you in ages."

Eli shook his hand. "Good to see you, sir."

"What brings you to town?"

"Helping my parents out with a few things. They're selling the house."

"Oh, I heard. You're such a good son."

Eli smiled, and I hated the way I felt a flutter when he did. "Plus, my ten year high school reunion is coming up."

Alex smiled and looked at me. "Is that right? Well, I hope I'll see more of your class come on in here. Don't tell the others, but your class was my favorite."

Eli said, "You say that to all the classes."

Alex flitted a hand at him and laughed. "Do you want your usual table?"

We both laughed. "You remember where we used to sit?" I asked.

"Of course," Alex said, grabbing two menus and walking us over to the table by the corner window. "I still think it looks kind of weird when anyone else sits here. You better come on over to say hi to my wife before you leave." He set the menus down on the table. "She'll be very angry if she finds out you were here and didn't talk to her."

"Of course," Eli said. "Thank you, sir."

Alex wandered back to the host stand.

"So," Eli said, "don't tell me that you don't come here anymore."

"I do, I swear! I'm just usually taking an order to-go unless I'm with my parents or Paige or something."

Eli glanced over at the edge of the table where the napkins, condiments and a cup of crayons sat. He smirked at me, then started rolling up the sleeves of his white button-down shirt.

Alex's was one of those places that put a sheet of paper over the table so that little kids could draw on it. Eli and I had always used to cover our table. When we were younger, it was silly drawings or games of hangman or tic-tac-toe. When we got older, we used it to study, writing out long calculus equations or listing everything we could remember about the French revolution. The occasional doodle still slipped in. Alex had always said that we used those sheets of paper more than anyone else, that we were going to put him out of business by using up so much paper and ordering too many milkshakes.

"Oh my gosh," I said, "you're not really going to draw something, are you?"

He scoffed. "Of course I am. At Alex's, it's mandatory."

"It is not."

"Where's your sense of adventure, April? Are you really going to let me create a masterpiece in isolation?"

I snorted. "Masterpiece?"

"Hey, I took, like, one art class in college. You don't know what I'm capable of anymore."

"Fine," I said, grabbing a menu and propping it up in between us so that we couldn't see each other's drawing. "Three minutes. No peeking. No theme. Best drawing wins."

"Wins what?"

"I don't know. A milkshake?"

"I thought we were ordering those anyway."

"Loser pays?"

Eli tugged at his collar. "I'm already paying."

Eli was planning to pay? "Fine, bragging rights."

He snapped his finger. "Loser calls Quinn to tell her we booked the park."

"Oh, that's just evil!"

"Scared?"

I shook my head and grabbed my phone, setting a three-minute timer. "Three, two, one, go!"

We both immediately started scribbling, mostly ignoring each other except to accuse the other of peeking or hogging a certain crayon color. I was trying to focus on my drawing, but I couldn't stop overanalyzing everything that was happening. Eli had taken me to Alex's: that leaned friends. He had come expecting to pay: that leaned date. He'd brought up the reunion planning: that leaned friends. He was wearing a white button-down shirt and black pants: that leaned date. Eli challenged me to a drawing contest: that leaned friends. The way he kept looking at me over the top of the menu and smirking, and the way I had to force myself to stop looking at him every time he did it because if I kept looking I would totally forget to draw and become obsessed with what it would be like if Eli Forrester kissed me: well...

I shook my head and focused on the drawing. I was getting way ahead of myself. Eli was my friend, and he always had been. Sure, he was considering moving back to River Glen, but nothing was set in stone. I really had nothing to go off of that made this a confirmed date.

And what happened when Ryan got to town? Ryan had made it pretty clear that he wanted to get together. The way he had spoken sounded much more like a date than anything Eli had said. I was just letting myself get carried away because Eli was here and Ryan wasn't. Eli was my friend, and if I had anything to do about it, we would be friends for a long time. Once Ryan got here, I would go on a date with him and see what would happen. It was as simple as that.

My phone timer beeped, and Eli shouted, "Crayons down!"

I grabbed the menu but didn't lower it. "Are you ready?"

He scoffed. "Are you ready to lose?"

"Oh, so arrogant."

He held up a finger. "Confident, not arrogant."

I rolled my eyes. "Whatever. Three, two, one."

I tossed the menu aside and found that we had gone completely different routes with our drawings, and when I realized that he'd drawn a picture of me, all of the serious, rational decision-making I'd just done about Eli and Ryan went out the window. It was actually beautiful. It had a pop art vibe since he had used exclusively red and blue, but it was undeniably me. It was a crayon drawing done in three minutes, so it was no masterpiece, but I couldn't help but feel like I looked prettier in that waxy drawing on a stained tablecloth than I did in real life.

"I thought we were drawing each other," Eli said in exasperation.

"I said no theme."

"I thought that meant that we draw each other, not some dude on a horse."

"Some dude? Excuse you, but that is Ulysses S. Grant, thank you very much!"

"You had three minutes to draw a picture in crayon on a table with only three colors, and you chose a Civil War general?"

"So what if I did?"

He laughed. "It's a good thing you're a history teacher."

"What is that supposed to mean?"

"Just that you chose the right career path, that's all."

I pointed at his drawing of me. "And what about you? You didn't even use all three colors."

"That was intentional. I only used red and blue because it's patriotic. It's called symbolism, April. You love American history, so I picked American colors. Besides," he said, his voice shifting a little lower, "blue suits you."

Did I just see Eli's eyes flicker down to my dress? Was I totally losing my mind and hallucinating things? I had to be, right?

"Well, I think you hustled me," I said. "Obviously that art class you took taught you how to draw portraits in crayon. You had an unfair advantage."

"I told you about the art class. That's not hustling."

I pointed at my own drawing. "My horse is a stick figure. That doesn't even make any sense."

"Not my problem. Guess you're calling Quinn."

I folded my arms. "The park wasn't even my idea. It was yours."

"Sore loser."

I shoved his arm across the table, and he laughed. I'd always loved that laugh. It was so pure and honest, as warm as his arm was where I touched him. I always felt like you never had to wonder how Eli felt when he laughed because his laugh was so authentic. It was ironic now that I was spending a lot of time trying to figure out how Eli felt.

Our burgers came, and we ate while mostly talking about the reunion and occasionally reminiscing about high school. It was so easy with Eli. I always felt like myself around him, like I didn't have to pretend to be anything but me. In high school, when your worth as a person is so tied to how people perceive you, it had been refreshing to have a friend like Eli that I never had to be fake around. I trusted him implicitly, and I always felt like my best self around him.

After drinking one milkshake each and splitting a third, we paid Alex and headed out.

"That last milkshake was a mistake," I said.

Eli shook his head. "Still can't hold your milkshake, eh, April?"

I elbowed him gently. "Some of us don't eat like that every day."

"Oh no, don't tell me you're a health food freak now. That would cause some serious damage to our relationship."

Relationship? Was I totally insane to read too much into the use of that word over the word "friendship"?

"Want to walk for a while?" Eli asked. "It's not miserably hot outside right now. We could walk off some milkshake calories."

"Sure, but I'm not sure it'll do much at this point."

He shrugged. "Worth a shot."

We started walking around the park downtown, and I pictured our last day at the park, when Eli had helped me plan the reunion, when he had danced with me around the big tree. I could still feel the weight of his hand on my back, his fingers laced in mine. The feeling was so palpable that I didn't even notice when he had slipped his hand in mine, weaving our fingers together. The moment I realized that the feeling was real and not a memory, warmth radiated from where our palms touched. Just like that day in his parents' house, I found myself wishing that that contact would never end.

"So," he said without looking at me, just staring at the ground, "I talked to my parents about the house."

"Really? What did they say?"

"My mom was ecstatic. She tried to just give it to me, but I told her I would pay for it. Now if they wanted to give me a massive discount, I wouldn't say no."

I chuckled. "And your dad?"

He let out a long sigh. "I don't know. I think he likes the idea of my being close to home, but I think he's got that whole 'be your own man' mindset. I'm not sure buying your parents' house fits that mold for him."

"I mean, you became a dentist."

"Orthodontist," he said with a wink.

"Orthodontist. You didn't join the military or do law enforcement or something. That was your own thing. So was NYU."

"Yeah, I guess so. I don't know, I guess I just always worry that he's disappointed."

"He's definitely not. Every time I see him, he talks about you. He's proud of you."

"It's just not his style, I guess, to praise me."

I shook my head. "But it doesn't mean he doesn't think what you've accomplished is impressive. I remember when you started at NYU, he told anyone who would listen that his son got into NYU. He loved being able to brag about you."

He smiled, and it looked like the weight lifted off of his shoulders just the tiniest bit. "I was so homesick that first year."

"Really? It didn't seem like it."

"Oh yeah. There was no one else up there, and it took me a long time to find something to get involved in. It took forever to make any friends. I just missed River Glen so much. Everyone here knows everyone, you know? But in New York, I was just one of so, so many. I hated that."

"Must have been hard."

"It was," he said, but he seemed to want to say more. When I looked at his face, he stopped walking, so I did, too, and he looked straight into my eyes. "I didn't think I'd be up there alone."

There it was again. The guilt. The way I had abandoned the plan that Eli and I had for college and never told him why. Now it felt like too much time had passed to say anything. It just felt awkward to bring something up now that was ten years dead in the water.

"I mean," I said, "even if I had gone to Boston University, I wouldn't have been super close."

"Closer than Florida," he said sadly. He glanced down at our still intertwined hands then back up to my eyes. "You never told me why you changed your mind."

"I didn't really change my mind."

"What do you mean?"

I still didn't want to say, and that felt so silly. This was Eli of all people. Eli always understood, Eli was always there for me, Eli was always honest with me. Why did I think I had to keep something from him? It was childish, like we were still in high school. We were adults now, so why couldn't I act like it and tell him the truth?

"Things just changed. I still wanted to go to BU, but I had to choose in-state. It just made the most sense at the time."

"I just really missed—well, I missed you," he said, taking the smallest step toward me. I became aware of the fact that there weren't a ton of people around, and although we were in the park and totally visible, we weren't exactly surrounded by a crowd. No one would see if Eli kept moving closer to me or the way we were looking into each other's eyes.

"I missed you, too."

"You were the person I most missed while I was in New York. Don't tell my mom," he said with a laugh.

"Really?"

He nodded, then took another step closer. We were closer than we had been when we were dancing the other day. "You would have changed everything about my college experience if you had been there."

"You probably would have studied less."

He laughed again, and I could smell his cologne when he moved his neck: amber and burning wood. "That would have been all right."

"You might not be an orthodontist now if I had distracted you."

"Would have been worth it."

Suddenly, Eli's eyes were no longer staring into my eyes but staring at my mouth, and he had moved even closer, though I hadn't thought that possible. He was so close I could practically feel what was about to happen.

But what *was* about to happen? Was I really about to kiss Eli Forrester? Never in a million years would I have believed that if someone had told me. But I still felt bad about not being honest with Eli about Boston.

And suddenly, my head was spinning with fears: What if this wrecked our friendship? What if he was mad at me for never telling him the truth? What if he was moving back to River Glen for me? What if I was leading him on knowing I was going to go on a date with Ryan when he got to town? What if I hurt Eli a second time?

At the last second, just before his lips made contact with mine, I turned my head, and the ache it caused me was palpable. My stomach twisted, and I suddenly felt the need to hunch over from pain though of course I didn't. I so badly wanted to kiss him—so badly that I felt a lack of oxygen at his rejection. But I shouldn't want to kiss him. I had let myself get carried away, and I had to put a stop to it for both of us.

Eli looked surprised when I moved my head, and I hated the look in his eyes.

"I'm sorry," I said.

"It's okay," he said, though his voice made it sound like it really wasn't. "I shouldn't have—"

"No, I just—I didn't want to mess anything up."

He smiled slightly. "I wasn't worried."

"You mean a lot to me, Eli. You always have."

The smile grew. "Glad to hear it."

"I just don't think I'm ready to—"

"I totally get it," he said with a smile that didn't look as authentic as it did moments ago. He fidgeted with the hem of his shirt a little, snapped three or four times, then looked up and forced another smile. "Can I drive you home? We've probably walked off our milkshakes."

I nodded, and my stomach felt like it was twisting, and I knew it wasn't from the milkshakes.

October 20, 2013

Letter of Recommendation for April Corwin

To Whom It May Concern,

April Corwin stands out as one of the most exceptional students I've ever taught. Not only is she a driven, self-motivated student who is high-achieving and intelligent, but she is also a student who is always kind and always genuine, a rare combination in the adolescent high school student.

I have had April as a student for the past four years in my journalism class which produces the school newspaper, the RGA Tribune. Even when she was a freshman, I saw a great deal of potential in April due to her excellent work ethic. I never had to prompt her to work hard because it seemed to be her inherent nature. She worked up the ranks in the paper until she became editor-in-chief her senior year. What I have seen from April over the last four years is creativity, intellect, perseverance, optimism, and leadership. She often comes up with new ideas to make the paper more interesting to other students. She is an excellent writer herself, but she also knows how to motivate the underclassmen and help them become the best journalists they can be. She is well-respected by her peers because she is kind and helps without judgment or taking control. Her ability to teach and counsel her peers is exceptional—the kind of intuitiveness that cannot be taught but is innate.

I offer April my highest recommendation because she stands out as among the best of my students over a thirty-four year career. I have no doubt that she will be highly successful in college and beyond because she is a student with the right priorities. She has clearly defined goals, and I am confident that she will achieve anything she sets her mind to. I expect to see her have a significant impact in the lives of others.

Sue Gabler, M.A.
Elective Teacher (Journalism, Culinary, Yearbook)
River Glen Academy

11

The final bell of the day rang, and the students flooded rapidly out into the hallway. I didn't have Model UN meetings after school, so I was pretty excited that I could go home at a reasonable time. In an effort to protect my precious free time, I packed up my stuff quickly and bolted for the parking lot before anyone could see me and try to pull me into a meeting or just start chatting. I loved my coworkers, I really did, but I rarely had a night off after school between Model UN and student government, so I had to make the most of it when I did. My leftovers from yesterday and a devil's food donut from Paige were calling my name.

I turned down the main hallway and was surprised to see Eli standing there talking to Mrs. Gabler. Mrs. Gabler was our teacher in high school. She taught a million different electives, and we used to joke that it would take three or four people to replace her when she retired because she had so many random skills. She was part-time now—partially retired—and it had already taken two more part-time teachers to cover the gaps. She was always one of my favorite teachers because she was so kind and so genuinely good at what she did. Looking at the way Eli smiled when he talked to her, I assumed she must have been one of his favorites, too.

"Who let you on campus?" I said as I walked over to them. "We've got to do something about the security here."

Mrs. Gabler laughed, and Eli feigned shock. "Hey, I was going to wait outside, but Mrs. Gabler insisted I come in. I'm not the one to blame here."

"Well, I had to let in my top culinary student so I could say hello," she said with a sweet smile.

Eli sighed dramatically. "Ah yes, my culinary achievements. I doubt I'll ever achieve a comparable accomplishment."

I rolled my eyes. "Oh my gosh."

"You're just mad that you weren't the top student in culinary."

"Oh yes, I've been long harboring that resentment toward you."

"Oh, it's all right," Mrs. Gabler said. "You were my top journalism student."

"Good to know."

"Speaking of, how is your thesis coming along, dearie? You'll have to let me read it once it's done."

"It's actually going well," I said, and for the first time, I felt like I actually meant it. "I'm almost done. I'll let you read it after I pass my defense, how's that?"

She chuckled. "Very well." She turned to Eli. "Well, it was very nice to see you, young man. Say hello to your parents for me."

"I will. Bye, Mrs. Gabler."

Mrs. Gabler slipped back into her classroom, and Eli and I started walking out of the building together.

"So what are you doing here?"

"I have news," he said. "Want to take a walk? We could stop for coffee or something."

"Sure," I said, but I wondered where this was leading. We weren't near downtown, so the only thing that was really nearby was the one

Starbucks in town unless he was planning to walk all the way to the one little strip mall that was at least a twenty minute walk. I dropped off my bag in my car, and we started walking.

I also wondered where this was leading metaphorically. What news did he have? We hadn't talked since a couple of nights ago when he almost kissed me and I stopped him. I still kind of regretted stopping him, but what if kissing Eli ruined everything? What if our friendship was never the same again?

What if I moved away?

He was seriously considering moving back to River Glen, and I was still thinking about moving to Boston at some point. But what point was that? If it hadn't happened in the last ten years, was it ever going to? But could I risk hurting Eli, who was planning a life and a family here, by moving to Boston now after not moving to Boston when he wanted me to?

Eli said, "So I have three pieces of news."

"Three?"

"Yes. First of all, I called Emma, and she sent me an email with all of the fun things she planned for the reunion. She had a list of our old superlatives, so I figured we could make a slideshow or something out of those."

"That's fun."

"Yeah. Plus she had some ideas for videos we could show or trivia games we could play. They weren't super fleshed out or anything because she hasn't had time to work on them, but the ideas are good. I figured we could knock them out."

"Oh, definitely. We could maybe twist Paige's arm into helping, too."

He snorted. "That's a big maybe."

"And Ryan would probably be willing to help, too. When he's in town, at least."

The corner of his mouth twitched. "Right."

Why did he react like that every time I mentioned Ryan? Ryan wasn't even here. Of course, he would be soon, and I wondered how that would change the dynamic here. Was Eli jealous of Ryan? I had thought people got over those kinds of things once high school ended, but I guess for me, high school never really had ended.

"So, what's next?" I asked.

He brightened. "Well, I canceled my lease at the apartment I've been renting. I'm officially buying my parents' house."

"Wow, really?" When Eli had first told me about the house, it had seemed like the most natural option. It was so easy to picture him there, and I assumed he would buy it, but I didn't really think about what it would mean when he actually did it, when it was actually a reality. Eli was moving back to River Glen. For good.

He nodded. "Since this isn't a typical sale, there's really no reason for me to wait until they move out to move in. So I'm moving my stuff this weekend. That way, I can help my parents finish packing what's left. It'll be way easier this way."

"So those boxes your mom made you take are just going right back to the house?"

He laughed heartily. "Yeah, I pointed that out, too. She didn't think it was as funny as I did."

The wind was whipping my hair around, so I pulled it to the side and tied it off. "Wait a second. So you just bought a house? Like a whole house? Isn't that kind of a financial hit?"

"Not really. I didn't exactly pay full price for it."

"Still."

"And I'm not paying for the apartment anymore. I'll have to buy some new furniture since my parents are taking a lot of it, but it's not terrible."

"But you're not even working right now. I'm sorry, maybe this is my teacher salary talking, but can you afford that right now?"

"Well, then I guess it's a good thing that I got a job at Steiner Orthodontics," he said with a wide grin.

"No way, Steiner?" We had both gotten our braces at Steiner. Pretty much everyone in River Glen did. There were some other orthodontists that people went to in Orlando, but a lot of the community had always gone to Dr. Steiner.

"Yeah. I had an interview last week. I didn't tell you because I had no idea if I even had a shot. He wasn't even advertising that he had an opening. I just kind of showed up and asked if I could have a job."

I laughed. "And he said yes."

He nodded. "Basically. He said he's been trying to cut back on hours and work toward retirement, but the other orthodontist there Dr. Denner is already slammed and can't take on any more patients. Plus, she doesn't do pediatric orthodontics, and since that's most of what Dr. Steiner handles, it just didn't make sense."

"Wow, that's so great."

"He was actually really enthusiastic about it. He wanted to cut back, but he didn't want to leave Dr. Denner stranded. He said I was exactly the solution he needed. I don't start for another couple of weeks so that I can help my parents out and finish the house, but it's all falling into place."

It was falling into place, and somehow, that was unsettling to me. Eli was doing everything he wanted to do. He had wanted to go to dental school, and he had at his first choice school. Now he was specialized and managed to land the perfect job and the perfect house.

He was going to make kids giggle and smile while he straightened their smiles and set up his new house to be the perfect family home—something it already was, but now he was going to make it his own. Eli was succeeding at absolutely everything he ever wanted from high school to now.

And what was I doing? I hadn't gone to my first choice school, and I wasn't in the job I had planned or the city I loved. My entire plan had crumbled before me over the last ten years, and something about seeing Eli succeed made me feel like even more of a failure. Sure, my dad's accident had set me back, and sure, Boston University's faulty financial aid calculations were out of my control, but I couldn't blame all of my failures on that. I hadn't worked hard enough to get scholarships to compensate. I had let myself become afraid of being alone in Boston wondering if my parents were okay. I had taken a job I hadn't really wanted at the time, and I had let myself get stuck in that job. I could have just moved to Boston and gotten a teaching job there. I could have reapplied for the Master's program there and taken the low pay and the free tuition. Why hadn't I done any of those things? Because I had already failed, and it felt stupid to try to cling to something that was already out of reach.

We were nearly at the Statbucks, but Eli stopped walking all of a sudden and faced me. "Hey, is everything okay? You got kind of quiet."

How long had I been spiraling? I wasn't even sure how long the silence had stretched between us as Eli tried to celebrate his happiness with me and I had totally shut down.

"Yes, sorry. I'm really happy for you."

He touched the side of my arm gently. "Are you sure you're okay?" I nodded, but he didn't seem convinced, so he gestured for us to sit on one of the benches behind Starbucks. "I feel like you're not being honest with me about something. Can we talk about it?"

Eli was always so perceptive, and he knew me too well. I had to be honest with him finally after all these years. We weren't in high school anymore: I had to grow up and actually talk through this with Eli instead of being weird and shutting him out.

"There's a reason I didn't go to Boston University after high school, and I never really told you about it."

He gave me a gentle smile. "I'm listening."

"You remember when my grandfather died?" I asked, and he nodded. "Well, he left my dad a lot of money, but he lost his job right after that, and he had a hard time finding another one. Luckily, we had that inheritance money to fall back on, but Boston University calculated my financial aid based on my dad's job and that inheritance, and they basically offered me nothing."

"Oh man," Eli said sympathetically. "That's so awful."

I nodded. "I didn't really talk about it because I was still so upset about my grandfather, and, I don't know, I guess I felt like a failure. I mean, you earned scholarships to afford NYU, and I just kind of assumed that the money would come through at BU, but it didn't. I was embarrassed that I couldn't go there after talking about nothing else for so long. That's why I went to FSU. I needed the in-state tuition."

"I mean, that makes sense. It doesn't make you a failure."

"But I reapplied for graduate school senior year of college, and I got in and was going to be a graduate teaching assistant to get free tuition, but then my dad got in that car accident."

"I remember my mom mentioning that."

"I just couldn't leave them and move to Boston, you know? Maybe that was more about me not wanting to leave them than it was about them needing my help, but I chickened out and stayed here. I knew

I could get a job teaching pretty easily, and it was supposed to be temporary, but I've just been stuck here for the past six years."

He took my hand in his, and while I was somewhat aware that he was just trying to be comforting, I once again really liked the way my hand felt in his and also felt like he didn't have to touch my hand to be comforting. "You're not stuck. You made decisions based on your priorities. There's nothing wrong with that."

"This just isn't how I pictured my life going. I pictured Boston and a professorship, not River Glen and my high school history classroom. It just seems like your life looks exactly how you imagined it, and I'm nowhere near it."

"I didn't always picture this life for myself. I was going to play soccer and maybe major in business or communications or something broad. Orthodontics came out of nowhere. And I definitely didn't think in high school that I'd move back to River Glen someday."

"But it makes so much sense for you."

"Maybe, but that's life. Sometimes our plans change, but it doesn't mean we've failed. We're just not the exact same people we were at seventeen years old."

I laughed. "Thank goodness, honestly."

"You chose to prioritize your family and your finances, and there's nothing wrong with doing that. It's good, even. And you're successful in your career, close to your parents, and still getting the Master's you wanted. Now how is that failure?"

When Eli said it, it sounded so much simpler. It was hard to let go of a life I had always wanted, but he was right: I was happy, and I was doing well. He put things in perspective for me.

"Thank you," I said. "That helps a lot."

He smiled to an almost cheesy point. "I'm glad." He hesitated, staring down at our intertwined hands, then finally looked up and said, "Can I ask you something though?"

"Sure."

"Do you still think about moving to Boston? Like are you still considering that?"

"I don't know," I said honestly. "It's what I always wanted, so I guess I do still think about it, but I'm really not sure what I want."

But Boston was feeling a little more distant by the day and not because it was out of reach but because maybe I wasn't reaching for it anymore. Maybe I needed to mourn that part of my life, but maybe I didn't hate the idea of staying in River Glen quite as much as I wanted to believe that I did. Didn't I like my job and my students? Didn't I like what I was researching for my Master's thesis? Was it really so bad?

And was staying in River Glen the wrong decision when it felt so right to sit here with Eli and hold his hand? I had always been comfortable around Eli, but this was different. I never should have stopped him from kissing me the other night. That was so stupid, and I had regretted it ever since. I liked Eli, and Eli liked me, and maybe that was enough. Maybe I was the one making things too complicated, like always. Maybe I needed to stop fighting my feelings or the way my head spun when I smelled his cologne or the way I wanted to kiss him just as much as I had wanted to before—maybe even more.

Eli wasn't really looking at me—it seemed like he was lost in his thoughts—so I slipped my free hand up to his chin and tilted his face toward me. Once again, just like the other night, his eyes dropped to my lips. My breath felt fluttery the longer he held his gaze. He started to lean in again, but this time, I wouldn't pull away.

But moments before our lips touched, Eli was the one to pull back. The disappointment that washed over me was much more devastating than the first time. The first time, I had been the one to back off out of respect for our feelings. Last time, he had been the one rejected; this time, it was me.

"I'm sorry, I—" Eli stopped and shifted back from me on the bench. "I shouldn't have tried to force it."

"You didn't—"

"You were probably right the other night. I'm sorry."

"It's okay," I said, though that was the furthest thing from the truth.

Corwin!

I never thought graduation would come! Even though we weren't super close, I've always thought you were pretty cool. I wish we had hung out more often, but I guess we were both pretty busy. I hope we can stay in touch in college. Good luck next year! I know you'll rock it!

Stay cool!
—Ryan Bennings #15

CLASS OF 2014

BYE BYE
-LUCA

Corwin, you were the best chem lab partner ever! Best of luck next year.
xoxo Lucy

Corwin,
You were a pleasure to have in class. Big things ahead!
Best, Mr. K

12

I walked down the main street of downtown somewhat aimlessly. I should have been finalizing details for the reunion or reading my thesis director's revision notes, but I couldn't help but take a walk to try to clear my head. Besides, in Florida, when it wasn't excruciatingly hot outside, you took advantage of it and spent as much time outside as humanly possible.

This street was pretty. The city hung some cute fall decorations to try to compensate for the lack of autumnal foliage in Florida, so there were orange and red leaf garlands wrapped around all of the streetlights. There were also string lights stretching across the main road connecting businesses across the street from each other. I didn't particularly care for fall, but River Glen did it right.

My phone buzzed in my bag, but between the latte I was holding and the stupid notebook I had brought because I thought I would take notes while I walked, I didn't get to it in time to answer the call. I stopped walking for a moment to see who it was, and I saw that I missed a call from Ryan. *Dang it.* I shoved my notebook under my chin, pinned my latte between my arm and my side, and tried to type out a "sorry I missed your call, were you calling to talk business about the reunion or to ask me out" chill sort of text, but halfway through, I heard someone laughing behind me.

"Ignoring my calls now, Corwin?" Ryan said, and I whipped around, nearly dropping phone, notebook, and latte all in one fell swoop. "That cuts me to the core."

"Ryan," I said in an attempt at being casual, but it came out louder than I intended. I shoved my notebook and phone in my bag and grabbed my latte, hoping the tiny bit that I felt spill went onto the pavement and not my clothing. "I was just replying. What are you doing here?"

"Am I not supposed to be here?"

"No, of course not, I—I just thought you weren't coming in until Thursday."

He shrugged, hands in pockets. Dang, he looked good. "Thought I'd come in earlier. I didn't want to miss all the festivities."

He held his arms out for a hug, and I hesitated for longer than I probably should have, but it was just so incredulous that Ryan Bennings of all people was actually offering me a hug right now. I hugged him carefully to avoid spilling my drink on his jacket—a jacket that seemed much too warm for Florida—and he gave me a squeeze that made me smile, but inside I felt kind of weird about it. Hadn't I just been hoping that Eli would kiss me?

But it was still hard to ignore the way I felt when Ryan hugged me. It felt so good in contrast to the somewhat chilly air. He smelled incredible, like he was wearing a pretty expensive cologne, and he chuckled slightly in my ear in a way that gave me goosebumps. When he leaned back, I took in his whole face. Obviously I'd seen it multiple times lately over our video chats, but seeing him in person was different. What I was learning was that video chat technology did not adequately communicate how attractive Ryan continued to be. He somehow looked the same but also better, like age had only improved his natural genetics. I realized that he was taller than I expected him to be, and I wondered if he'd grown or if this was how tall he'd always been, but I was never this close to him, his arms around me, his hands touching my back.

"Plus," he said, "I really wanted to see you."

And, that was it. Any semblance of cool I was trying to play to myself was gone. I was glad to see Ryan, and he was glad to see me. This was officially a thing.

"I'm glad," I said. "It's so good to see you." *Good, April,* I thought. *That was actually smooth.*

"What are you doing right now?" he asked, one hand still noticeably on my back.

What was I doing right now? Hyperventilating, procrastinating, questioning my life decisions, panicking?

"What am I doing?"

He laughed. "I mean, are you busy right now? Could we take a walk? Maybe get some coffee?" He looked down at the latte in my hand. "Maybe not coffee."

"This isn't coffee," I said. "It's a chai latte."

He hesitated. "So, no coffee, then?"

"No—I mean, yes—I mean—sure, let's go for a walk."

A wide smile. "Fantastic."

We started walking, and I wasn't really sure where we were headed or if he had something in mind, but I decided not to worry about it too much. Other than a couple of smiles in my direction, neither of us really acknowledged each other. It was a tad awkward.

"So," I said, attempting to break the silence, "are you staying in town?"

"Yeah, at the bed and breakfast on Mulberry. Have you ever been there?"

"No, but I remember when it was renovated a few years ago. How is it?"

"It's really nice."

Another moment of silence.

"Has it been long since you've been back in town?"

He nodded. "Several years, actually. My parents moved to Hawaii after I graduated from River Glen, so I don't come back to this area much."

"Hawaii?"

"Yeah. Crazy, right? They decided they could do whatever they wanted once I was out of the house. I don't know if I should be offended," he said with a laugh.

"I mean, I can't say I wouldn't move to Hawaii if I could."

He scrunched his nose, and it was kind of cute. "Not me. It's too tropical. I actually really like Boston. It's the perfect amount of city for me." He paused for a moment, then added, "That sounded weird, didn't it?"

"Not at all. I totally get it. I love Boston for the same reason. It's big enough to have big city benefits without feeling oppressively large or overwhelming."

"Exactly. It's just the perfect place. I don't think you ever really told me, but why didn't you end up in Boston? I thought I remembered hearing you were going to go to Boston University."

No, Ryan, we did not talk about it because I skillfully avoided that particular topic of conversation. "It just didn't work out. I needed to stay close to home, and in-state tuition was a lot more feasible."

"Oh that's totally fair. I'm still paying off student loans," he said with a chuckle. Every time he laughed, I couldn't help but smile. He had one of those infectious laughs that just made everyone around happy.

"Maybe one day I'll make it to Boston."

"I mean, teaching is a pretty mobile career, isn't it? You could move."

"Yeah, I could, but I wouldn't want to move without a plan. I have a good job. I'd have to find something much better to convince me to move."

As the words came out, I was surprised by them. A few years ago, I would have immediately moved to Boston at the suggestion and the opportunity. I guess I hadn't realized how attached I'd become to working at River Glen with those kids. And this town.

"I get that. Well, maybe after this is all over, you can come visit," he said, and I felt a flutter in my chest. "I'd love to show you around my favorite places in Boston."

"That sounds awesome. Maybe during a school break or something."

"It's a plan," he said. "So, I wasn't kidding about coffee earlier. I haven't had any since before my flight early this morning. Is there somewhere nearby?"

"Yeah, there's a shop just down here—" I stopped myself. I was going to suggest Paige's place, but I absolutely couldn't walk into Paige's shop with Ryan. She would cause a scene.

"There is?"

"Uh, yeah, but we could also—"

Ryan pointed right at the Donutisserie. "Is it that one?"

No getting out of it now. "Yes, that's it. It's actually owned by Paige."

"Paige?"

"Paige Somerville. From high school?"

"Right, of course. That's so cool that she opened her own coffee shop. Let's go. We can say hi."

That was exactly what I was afraid of. "Sure."

The whole time we walked toward the shop—which wasn't a long time since we were maybe two blocks away at most—I tried to strategize how best to approach this. Should I try to hide him from Paige? That seemed risky. If she caught me, she would definitely be mad at me. Should I just call Paige out and tell her he was here? That felt awkward. I guess I would just have to let it happen however it did.

Ryan opened the door, the chime jingled, and I inhaled sharply, bracing myself for Paige. Ryan walked up the counter and ordered a black coffee from the cashier, and I decided not to get anything—I didn't think I needed more caffeine right now.

I found a table somewhat hidden in a corner but not obviously hidden so that Paige couldn't accuse me of anything, and once Ryan got his drink, he joined me. He had barely sat down when I saw Paige come out of the inventory storeroom and freeze in her tracks. She very calmly set down the boxes she was carrying and walked over.

"That's Paige over there," I said to Ryan, pointing her out.

He spun around to see an extraordinarily calm and composed Paige walking toward him, the likes of which I had never seen. I expected a dramatic scene, but it appeared she was going to play it cool.

"Ryan," she said, a natural lilt in her voice, "is that you?"

"Paige Somerville!" he shouted, and several regular customers spun around to see what the commotion was all about. He gave her a hug, and I made careful note of the way he hugged her and the fact that it was different from the way he had hugged me. His hands seemed stiffer, and he didn't seem to lean in as much. "April was just telling me you opened your own shop."

"Was she now?" she said, giving me a look that went unnoticed by Ryan but that said so much to me. "Yes, I opened it about three years ago."

"That's so cool. River Glen's own entrepreneur."

"How about yourself? What have you been up to?"

"I work for an accounting firm in Boston. I've been there since I graduated."

Paige's expression was muddled by so many different emotions that I couldn't read her at all. "Really? Boston? What a coincidence. April loves Boston."

"Paige," I said between gritted teeth.

"We were just discussing that," Ryan said, smile wide. "I was trying to persuade her to let me show her around Boston sometime."

"Were you now? What an interesting turn of events," she said, and I made a mental note to berate her later for talking like a '40s movie star. "April, do you want to go visit Ryan in Boston?"

"I'm kind of in the middle of planning our reunion, you know. Plus, I have a job."

Paige held up a finger. "A job with a lot of breaks and days off. I think you could be convinced."

"I already said I would."

Paige looked surprised, but she covered it well enough. "You did?"

Ryan looked back and forth between us like he was desperately trying to figure out what secret code we were exchanging. Luckily, he completely misunderstood. "Somerville, do you want to come to Boston?"

He offered it genuinely, and I could tell that he would have been okay with Paige going, but I could also hear the slight edge of disappointment in his voice, like he was offering to be polite but he was really hoping she said no. I couldn't help but smile at the realization.

"Oh no," she said, "I'm way too busy with the shop. Besides, I'd just slow the two of you down." Only I caught the double meaning there; thankfully, Ryan was oblivious. "Well, I need to get back to work, but enjoy your coffee, Ryan. I'll see you at some of the reunion events, I'm sure."

"I thought you weren't going," I said. All she'd done for days was claim that she refused to attend our reunion.

"Oh, I wouldn't miss it for the world."

Paige walked away, but I could tell that she was still watching us from behind the counter. I politely excused myself and followed her to the counter.

"What is wrong with you?" I said in a loud whisper.

"Me? What is wrong with you? So now you're going to Boston with Ryan?"

"You're the one who said I should."

"If it's what you want." When I didn't answer, she added, "Is that what you want?"

"I don't know. Maybe it is."

"What about Eli? Did you guys have a date the other night?"

"It was not a date," I said, but immediately, I thought of how close he had come to kissing me, how I had pulled away.

"I hope you know what you're doing," Paige said.

I rejoined Ryan, but I noticed that Paige was still watching us from the counter. I tried to gesture to her to go away, but I couldn't do it without being obvious and Ryan asking why I was flinching like a weirdo. Plus, I didn't think that she had any intention of moving.

***

"So, are you thinking dance floor here?" Ryan said with his arms stretched out under the big lighted tree in the park, and I couldn't help but think about how Eli had done the exact same thing when we visited the park. It seemed impossible not to compare them, which seemed like a wildly ridiculous thought to have. Ryan Bennings and Eli Forrester were not comparable and never had been. They were so vastly different that the thought of trying to compare them forced me to stifle a laugh that rose in my throat. Still, there was the image of Eli in my head even as I stared into Ryan's face, a bright smile and an imposing figure.

I nodded and indicated other areas of the park. "And the catering table there, the dessert table there, and I was thinking we could set up the check-in table right here since it's closest to the parking lot."

"Yeah, that makes sense," Ryan said. "I think we should probably plan to have a table somewhere to set up the game stuff, too. Otherwise, we'll be lugging it all over the park."

I laughed, but before I could answer, the one and only Quinn Pendleton seemed to teleport magically into the center of the park. The park was in the center of downtown with nothing surrounding it except for the other buildings on the downtown streets, so it was nearly impossible to walk into the park without being noticed. Somehow, though, Quinn had managed to pull it off.

"We will definitely need a large table for games. I have a lot of ideas, and it's going to require a lot of equipment. We're going to need a sound system, some poster displays, a light-up game show wheel—"

"Do you already have all of this stuff?" I asked. "Because our budget is pretty much spent on food and the other stuff we already got."

Quinn scrunched her face. "So we're not even getting a sound system?"

"I mean, we'll have a DJ, so I'm sure you could borrow a mic from them for the games."

She huffed. "It's bad enough we're having this in the park."

"The park is beautiful, and it was the right price," Ryan added.

"That'll do, I guess. And the other things?"

"Best I can do is a table," I said.

She rolled her eyes, but thankfully, she moved on. "Okay, well I want to make some opening statements once everyone arrives."

"Opening statements?"

"Yes," she said as if I should have obviously understood her madness. "You know, welcome the class, tell some fun memories, and so on."

"That sounds like something the class president should do."

"Well, our class president isn't coming, now is she? Someone has to pick up the slack."

"Then shouldn't it be the class vice president?" I said, gesturing in Ryan's direction. He laughed when I said it, and though he tried to suppress it, it didn't go unnoticed by Quinn who tried to disguise her annoyance by flitting her eyelashes at him.

"Of course Ryan should handle it, but I am happy to help."

"Thanks Quinn," Ryan said, but there was something just a tad ingenuine about it that made me smile.

Before Quinn could continue her tirade, my phone rang, and when I saw Eli's name on the caller ID, I stepped aside and answered.

"Hey, what's up?"

"Hey," he said, "I was running some errands for my parents, and one of them requires me going to FencePost."

I laughed. FencePost was this home goods store downtown that Eli's mom was obsessed with. It had been there forever, and the same older lady still ran it. It was a lot of knick knacks and cutesy things, and in high school, Eli and I had gotten really good at identifying things in random people's houses as being from FencePost.

"I'm surprised she didn't want to go there herself," I said.

"Oh, that's actually exactly why she sent me. She was trying not to blow the budget there."

"That's actually smart," I said, and I noticed Quinn tapping her foot with impatience. She didn't care what I thought, so I wondered why she even bothered to wait out my phone call.

"Well, since it's in the area, I thought maybe I'd drop by the park. You said you were going over there today to wrap up some plans, right?"

I lowered my voice. "Yeah. Quinn's actually here right now shooting torpedoes at everything we've come up with."

He laughed. "Of course she is. Okay, I'll be there in a few. I'll run through FencePost really fast and then walk over."

"Okay, see you soon."

I rejoined Ryan and Quinn and found her talking his ear off about some pep rally game we used to play in high school that she wanted to recreate at the reunion. I couldn't think of anything worse. I hadn't exactly enjoyed pep rallies in high school, so why would I want to relive one?

"Would people really want to play that game?" Ryan asked. "I mean, why would people want to?"

"For the nostalgia, Ryan, that's why," Quinn said. "Don't you want to feel the nostalgia?"

"Isn't that the whole point of the reunion itself?" he said sheepishly.

"Ugh, Ryan, just trust me."

He turned to me and smiled, and I felt warm all over. "Hey, all good?"

I nodded. "It was just Eli. He's in the area, so he's stopping by to help."

Quinn scoffed. "Do you guys even want my help?"

Ryan smiled his classic, charming, all-American smile that made everyone melt. "I think we've got a handle on it, Quinn, but thanks so much for offering! We'll call you if we need something."

I could practically see her face turning red, but she fought the urge to blow up—surely because it was Ryan who had said that to her and not me—and instead mumbled some excuse about being really busy and left.

After she was out of hearing range, Ryan turned his smile on me and said, "Do you think I said the wrong thing?"

I laughed. "Anything we could have said that wasn't 'Yes, Quinn, we'll do whatever you want' would have been the wrong thing."

Ryan leaned back against one of the small trees and stuck his hands in his pockets. "Do you ever look back on high school and wonder why your friends were who they were? I think about that a lot. I don't even mean that in a negative way, but just like, what draws you to people when you're in high school?"

"I do think about that, actually. Paige and I are still best friends, but we didn't have that many classes together, so it's kind of surprising that we became friends back then."

"See, that's what I mean. In high school, everything is about who you have the same schedule of classes with or who you were on a team with. That doesn't necessarily translate to real life, you know? Like, why weren't we better friends in high school?"

Before I could stop myself, I heard myself say, "Because you were popular, and I wasn't." I immediately regretted saying it as soon as the words were out, but it was honest, and it was true. Still, that understanding didn't do anything for my reddening cheeks.

To my surprise, Ryan laughed. "That's ridiculous."

"It is not."

"Of course it is. I wasn't popular."

"Ryan, you were the most popular person in our grade. Everyone loved you."

He smiled a little sadly. "Everyone loved how well I played football. That was it. I didn't have very many friends in high school that were real. That's why I don't really talk to a lot of people from River Glen anymore. You're lucky you had Paige and Eli. They're the real deal."

I nodded because it was true. Paige and Eli had always been real friends.

"I just wonder what high school could have been like if I hadn't been such a slave to the status quo politics."

I laughed loudly. "'Status quo politics' is the greatest phrase I've ever heard to describe high school."

He laughed, too. "But it's accurate, isn't it? I mean, you're such a great person, and I always knew that. I always wanted to make an effort to get to know you better, but I chickened out. Look at what I almost missed out on."

I became aware that at some point he had moved closer to me, and the lack of distance between us was now noticeable. Some part of me was still my high school self quaking at the fact that I was standing so close to Ryan, that he was talking about wanting to get to know me, but the adult me wondered if this wasn't exactly what I wanted.

In high school, Ryan was a teenage crush, and that was all. I didn't really know him, but I had that weird kind of obsession teenage girls always have over the cute guy in their grade, and for whatever reason, they're usually on the football team. But now—well, we weren't in high school anymore, and we were getting to know each other better, and my feelings hadn't changed. No, that wasn't accurate. My feelings *had* changed because now they were mature, adult feelings. Ryan was educated, successful, driven, handsome, kind, and funny. He was everything I had always wanted. I thought about how rare a moment like this must be, that the high school crush turned out to have lasting impact and meaning. So often, the books and the movies show the high school crush growing up to be a loser or an average guy that doesn't offer that wow factor, but real life was so different. Here was Ryan, and he was everything I had hoped he would be and more.

"You know," I said, "I wasn't super thrilled when my boss asked me to plan this reunion."

"Mr. Quentin?" he asked, and I nodded. "He seems like an intense guy."

"He is, and I didn't think I really had time to do this. But I'm really glad I did."

"Yeah?"

I nodded again. "It meant reconnecting with you."

He smiled and took another step toward me, and I couldn't help but feel giddy as he got closer. "Glad to hear it."

"Even if Quinn has to intrude occasionally."

He let out a small laugh, and I liked the way the corners of his mouth turned up when he did. "I'd put up with Quinn for you."

I couldn't help but think about how easy this felt compared to Eli. Ryan was making it pretty clear where he stood with me, and surprisingly, I wasn't finding myself wondering what he was thinking. Some small part of me thought I must be delirious to think Ryan Bennings was interested in me, but I knew that I wasn't. Ryan was the kind of guy who made a girl feel confident about his feelings, and I liked that. This felt different than other relationships I'd had. Ryan felt like a real man who was being honest about what he wanted, and I liked that feeling.

Everything with Eli had been so difficult at every turn. He would seem like he just wanted to be friends, and then he would ask me on a date. Then we'd go to the diner we always used to go to, and that felt distinctly like friend territory. Then he was rejecting a kiss.

I didn't know where I stood with him, but seeing the way that Ryan was looking at me didn't make me question Ryan's feelings.

Maybe this was why nothing with Eli ever worked right. Maybe I was trying too hard to make something work that just wasn't meant to work. Maybe Eli and I were better off as friends, and trying to force something else was only hurting both of us. Everything just felt so easy with Ryan.

As we leaned in, I got the distinct feeling like we were about to kiss, and somehow, I knew that neither of us planned to pull away. But before he could get close enough, the sound of someone clearing his throat interrupted. We both snapped back from each other, and I turned to see Eli standing there.

"Eli," I said.

He forced a smile. "Just finished at FencePost. Am I interrupting?"

What a stupid question that was. Of course you were interrupting, Eli. But did he know what he had just interrupted? How obvious had we looked? I mean, we were just standing in the park, right? Maybe it didn't look the way it felt. But when I looked over at Ryan who was rubbing the back of his neck nervously, I felt pretty certain that it had looked exactly the way it had felt.

"Not at all," Ryan said. "Glad you could join us. You just missed Quinn, though."

"Somehow I think I'll go on."

Ryan and I both laughed, but Eli didn't, and everything felt strange now. Eli was the one to reject me at Starbucks the other day, so what right did he have to get jealous or angry now? Sure, it was awkward timing, but wasn't he out of line?

I said, "Quinn was just trying to convince us to play that game we used to play in pep rallies. Do you remember that?"

"Yes, and that's a terrible idea."

"See, that's what I'm saying," Ryan said, giving Eli a friendly slap on the back. "Glad to have you on my side."

Eli smiled, but I thought it looked more like a grimace. "So, what's the alternative then?"

"I don't know," he said. "This isn't exactly my forte."

"Emma sent a list of game ideas," I said. "We could look through those. They can't be worse than what Quinn came up with, right?"

Ryan seemed about to answer, but his phone chimed before he got a chance. He checked the screen and then sighed. "Sorry, gang, I've got to make a work related call. It might take a while. April, maybe we can catch up tomorrow?"

I nodded. "Sure."

He flashed a smile. "Okay, great. I'll text you. See you later, Eli."

Eli waved, but Ryan had already turned around and headed off, dialing on his phone. There was an awkward silence between the two of us which felt so foreign to our friendship but which had become increasingly common over the years. We barely even spoke for a while because of it. I had thought we had finally gotten past it, but it seemed that Ryan had reignited the tension.

Eli said suddenly, "Do you still need help, or did you and Ryan figure it out?"

It seemed that Ryan and I had, in fact, figured it out, but Eli had ironically interrupted it. "I think we got it, but we still need to pick games. Want to get together and go over it? I think Ryan likes pretty much all of them, so we need to narrow it down."

"Sure," he said, but it felt more than a little tense.

RYAN BENNINGS ALL STAR

By Quinn Pendleton

"FROM THE MOMENT HE STEPPED ON THAT FIELD, I KNEW HE WAS SOMETHING SPECIAL."

Coach Johnson said that he knew that senior Ryan Bennings was a standout player from his first tryout as an eighth grader. "Bennings was just that kind of memorable kid," Coach Johnson said. "From the moment he stepped on that field, I knew he was something special. There are some things you can't teach in football, and Bennings just had that 'it' factor."

It's that special quality that has led the Panthers to the state seminfinals the last three years. When asked about this year's run for the the state finals, Ryan Bennings had this to say: "I just want to play the game, you know? At the end of the day, I have to play my best if I expect us as a team to play our best. I know we've got the skills to get to the finals. I just hope I can play a role in getting us there."

Ryan's leadership is a huge factor as well. He became starting quarterback during his junior year, and he's become somewhat of a veteran on the varsity team. Several other football players noted that he is inspirational to them on and off the field. "He's just the kind of guy you want to follow into battle," junior Evan Young said. "He makes you want to play the game and win." Similarly, sophomore David Gent said, "If anyone can get us to the state competition, it's Ryan. He works so hard every day."

Time will tell if the Panthers get to that coveted state final spot, but one thing is certain: Ryan Bennings is the secret weapon.

13

— · —

I met up with Ryan the next day after school. I was tired, and if it had been any other day, I would have relished the idea of going straight home with some takeout food to watch a rom-com, but knowing that I was going to see Ryan gave me a bit of an energy boost.

We had agreed to meet at a local party supply store so that we could shop around for some decorations and decide what we liked. Quinn was sure to be furious if she found out we got decorations from a place that also sold Halloween costumes for children, but unlike Quinn, we were determined to stick to the budget Mr. Quentin had given us.

"What do you think about this?" Ryan asked as he pointed at a centerpiece display. It was the right color scheme—blue and gold—but it was pretty large, and it had stiff streamers sticking out in every direction.

"I think it might be too big," I said. "The tables we'll have at the park are not very big."

"But they're festive," he said with a smile.

"Sometimes subtlety is a good thing, you know."

"I don't do anything halfway, Corwin."

He winked, but something about spending all of this time with Ryan was still so bizarre. Ryan was the kind of guy in high school who was super nice and friendly with everyone, but because he was popular, he and I were not friends—high school rules dictated that we could not hang out. I didn't blame Ryan for that—high school was vicious in its adherence to status quo social standards—but I wondered what that would look like as adults now. Could we overcome that division? Had we not already found our way to each other?

"You know," Ryan continued, "I'm really glad we've gotten to reconnect because of this reunion."

"So you've said."

"Sure, but we kind of got interrupted," he said, and I thought about Eli showing up at the park yesterday. "I wanted to finish our conversation."

"Go on."

"You are definitely someone I always wished I had been closer with in high school."

"Really?"

I felt my face warm a little, and I could only hope that I wasn't actually blushing in any way that Ryan would be able to notice. To my surprise, he was the one who blushed.

"Yeah. I actually—I kind of had a crush on you in high school."

"Oh come on, you're making that up."

He laughed. "Not at all. You were always so interesting. I mean, obviously you're beautiful, but you were so confident and comfortable with who you were. I never was. Sometimes I still feel like I haven't figured out how to be confident in who I am."

"Are you serious? You were the most confident guy in our class. Quarterback, vice president—"

"I was good at faking it, but I was so unsure of myself. I didn't have any idea about what I wanted to do after I graduated. Everything was so football focused, and I got offers to play in college, but what did that really mean? I didn't know what to study when I got there."

"I mean, it seems like you figured it out."

He held up a bag of paper confetti. "What about this?"

"Yeah, grab like five or six of those."

He tossed them in the cart, and we kept roaming aisles. "I guess I did, but I took the long way. You always knew exactly what you wanted, and you went after it. I always admired that."

I'd known what I wanted, but I hadn't achieved it. Ryan was being nice, but he really didn't know how complicated that whole situation had become.

"I don't know if I would say that I was confident in high school," I said. "Everything I did was to impress somebody: my parents, my teachers, college admissions committees, everyone. I don't think I really was confident in myself." I laughed. "I guess we were all faking it in high school."

Ryan laughed heartily. "I think that's just high school, honestly. We're all just kind of winging it."

"Probably," I said with a chuckle.

"But seriously, one of my many regrets from high school is that I didn't make an effort to get to know you better. I might not be the smartest guy around, but I don't like to make the same mistake twice."

"What do you mean?"

He stopped walking so abruptly that I nearly crashed into the edge of the cart he was pushing. "April, would you like to have dinner with me?"

Ryan Bennings just asked me on a date. Oh, if only I could have told my teenage self that this would actually happen and not just be the product of some weird daydream.

"Dinner?"

He nodded. "I'm in town for a little while, and maybe we could have dinner and, you know, talk about something other than center-pieces and menus for the reunion."

I laughed, but I found myself oddly paralyzed and unable to answer. Before too much time passed, I forced myself to answer, "Yes, I'd love to."

He smiled wide, and it was funny to see how Ryan's smile still looked the same as it had in high school and yet looked more mature, like I could see his adolescent face in his older more manly expression. "Great. How's Thursday? Friday will probably be crazy with the alumni football game."

Thursday nights were my nights to have dinner with my parents, but that was so unofficial. It wasn't like it was a planned thing. I could not go one Thursday night. My parents would totally understand. They would be happy for me, even. I guessed I just hadn't realized how much of a habit that had become in my life. It felt weird to consider not going. But I certainly wasn't going to miss a date with Ryan Bennings of all people to play Scrabble with my parents. After all, they'd be there next week, and so would I.

"That works for me."

"Great," he said. "Can't wait. I'll pick you up at 6. What do you say we check out and get out of here? I don't think we're going to find anything else we like."

"Agreed."

As we headed to the cashier to buy the decorations we had found, I marveled at how wild life could be. My life looked so different from how I had imagined, but somehow, the most unlikely pipe dream part of it—a date with Ryan Bennings—was the one part that was actually a reality.

***

The next day, Eli and I met up at the Donutisserie to hash out some details. Emma had sent us some ideas for some reunion games to play, and while I thought they were all cheesy, I also understood that I wasn't exactly the target audience for those kinds of things. I enjoyed high school, but I really had no desire to see if anyone had lived up to their superlatives or future predictions, and I didn't want to try to guess who in our class had the most kids or who had the most unusual job. As the high school teacher who was unmarried and without kids, I wasn't exactly a standout.

Still, I doubted whether or not anyone would want to dance despite Eli's insistence that they would, so I wanted to have some fun activities as a backup. Ryan had already said he liked all of them, so Eli and I decided to weed out a few of the ones that were less interesting.

"We've got to trash this one," Eli said, tapping his pencil on my handwriting on the paper in the center of the table. "It's basically Bingo."

"But it's themed Bingo," I said. "It's like a guessing game. It'll be fun."

"April, it's our ten year reunion, not our fiftieth. We're not old people."

"Bingo is fun for all ages."

"That's the dumbest thing you've ever said."

"Oh come on, ever? Surely I said dumber stuff in, like, seventh grade."

"Okay fine," Eli said, sipping his coffee, "it's the dumbest thing you've said as an adult."

"Eh," I said, "still debatable."

He waved a hand at me. "Whatever. We'll put this one on the backup list."

"So far, we've put everything on the backup list. We haven't actually picked any games."

"Maybe that's a sign that we shouldn't have any games."

"Then are you going to take the responsibility when the reunion is lame and everyone's bored?"

"No one is going to be bored."

Paige walked over with refills of our drinks and rolled her eyes. "Oh my gosh, listen to the two of you. It's just like high school."

"What is that supposed to mean?" I asked.

"You guys always bickered like this in high school."

Eli said, "We did not."

"Oh my goodness, yes you did. Sometimes I wondered how you two were ever friends as much as you fought."

"Hey, this is friendly," I said waving my hand between Eli and me. "This is collaboration."

Paige waved her hands in both of our faces. "This is madness. And just like in high school, I'm sneaking out before the two of you can suck me into it."

With a smirk and flit of her hand, Paige was off to the stock room. Eli and I laughed, but one look between us, and I could tell that we both still felt the tension. Eli cleared his throat a couple of times, and I hated that I could feel my cheeks getting hot.

Eli had tried to kiss me. I had tried to kiss Eli. Neither attempt had actually resulted in a kiss. And now it was weird. If we made eye contact for longer than a normal interaction, we both immediately looked away. It seemed like we were both being cautious about not touching each other by accident. I was overthinking every word and every action around him, and I could have been wrong, but it felt like maybe he was doing the same thing. I couldn't help but wonder if we would ever get over this.

"Okay fine," I said, "Bingo goes on the backup list."

"Thank you."

"So what about the superlatives one?"

"I think that one's a classic. I'm pretty sure every high school reunion does that one."

Emma had sent us a list of our senior superlatives and future predictions as if we didn't all have them from the yearbook. It was kind of fun to look back at them and see how few of them had actually happened. I wondered if that was the case with all high school superlatives. Did any of them actually work out? Why were all high school seniors bad at guessing what their classmates would become? I guessed some of them were true at the time, but now they seemed kind of silly.

"We could start with that one," Eli said. "It's an easy one to do."

"Okay, hear me out," I said. "Superlative Bingo."

With a very serious face, Eli put both of his hands on mine and said, "You need to let go of the Bingo dream."

I laughed, but I couldn't ignore the feeling of his hands on mine. It was a normal touch, and I knew that he didn't mean anything by it, but I couldn't ignore the fact that it seemed that Eli and I couldn't just casually touch each other anymore. Every touch was charged now. As if reading my thoughts, he suddenly pulled away, suppressing the connection I know we both felt.

"Fine," I said. "Deprive the people of Bingo if you must."

I felt a little sad at the chill that overtook my hands when he was no longer touching them with his warmth, a warmth that was both physical but also the warmth of his personality. But Ryan's smiling face when he asked me out kept pushing its way forward, forcing me to acknowledge the fact that I was going on a date with Ryan. I had to stop thinking about Eli like that.

"Thoughts on the Jeopardy game?"

"Ryan likes that one, so we should keep it."

Ryan had found this customizable Jeopardy game with trivia questions based on everyone. We'd sent a Google form to our classmates to fill out with questions. Ryan and I had already put a lot of work into making it.

"Okay," Eli said. "We'll need some kind of buzzers or something."

"Ryan and I picked some up yesterday at the party supply store. We also got the mini whiteboards for the answers."

"You guys went to the store?"

I nodded. "We had to pick up some cheap decorations, and we found some other fun stuff there, too."

"Oh. Nice."

"It was actually Ryan's idea. He texted me and asked for some help after volunteering to handle decorations. And it's a good thing I did because he almost bought these massive blue streamer things and football decor. Not exactly the vibe."

He laughed, but it felt really forced, and I noticed him shifting a little. This had become a constant thing ever since Ryan had gotten into town. Eli hadn't been subtle about how much he disliked Ryan being involved, but Ryan was the one involved from the start. He was vice president, after all. Eli was only helping because I'd asked him to. It was weird for him to expect me to exclude him.

But was that what he was doing? Or did he just still hate Ryan because of whatever high school rivalry? I'd always heard people older than me say that high school never really ends, and I used to think that meant that people are always people and that people never really changed, but now I wondered if it didn't mean this. Maybe high school never ended because high school feuds and feelings never went away.

I decided to call Eli on it. I mean, things were definitely awkward, but Eli and I had trusted each other so deeply for so many years. In spite of current circumstances, surely he would be honest with me. I had to believe that if he could be honest, we could get past the uncomfortable air.

"What is it?" I asked.

"What do you mean?"

"It seems like something is bothering you."

"I'm fine," he said, but he tapped the edge of the table hard enough that the spoon next to his empty plate that once had a jelly donut rattled.

"You're not fine. Eli, I've known you for forever. What's bugging you?"

He sighed. "Ryan just gets on my nerves, that's all. It's not a big deal."

"Why does he get on your nerves?"

"He always has." Eli slumped in his chair. "He's just always so full of it."

"He's not really."

Eli sat up suddenly. "What makes you say that?"

"I think you just haven't really talked to him. He's not arrogant. He's actually pretty humble."

He rolled his eyes. "I'm sure he wants you to think so."

"What's that supposed to mean?" I said as I folded my arms.

"Seriously, April? Nothing's changed since high school. He's still the quarterback, and you're still the girl obsessing over him."

"Excuse me?"

"Am I wrong?"

I looked around and realized we'd drawn the attention of some of the other customers in the Donutisserie, so I got up from the table and gestured for Eli to follow. I turned down the side alley next to the Donutisserie and waited for Eli to catch up.

"Are you seriously accusing me of being the high school girl drooling over the football player?"

"Aren't you?"

I took a step back. "That's really insulting, Eli. I'm a full-grown adult, not a teenage girl."

"So you're telling me you wouldn't jump at the chance to go on a date with Ryan if he asked you."

I folded my arms, but I knew I was still fidgeting with my fingers. "Why shouldn't I? He's a perfectly nice guy."

Eli spotted my fingers, raised his eyebrows suddenly, and let out a wry laugh. "Oh my gosh. He did, didn't he? He actually asked you out."

"So what if he did?"

"Are you kidding me, April?"

"Hey," I said, holding up a finger, "you don't get to tell me who I can and cannot date. This isn't high school anymore."

"Well, apparently it is because you're still obsessed with him."

"I am not obsessed with him," I said so loudly it was almost a shout. When I realized people around us had noticed us, I lowered my voice. "He's a perfectly nice guy with a good career. Why shouldn't I go on a date with someone like that?"

"He doesn't live here anymore, you know. He lives in Boston. What are you going to do, move to Boston?"

"You're a little ahead of yourself. We haven't even gone on the date yet."

"Well I guess that's everything you ever wanted, right? Boston and Ryan Bennings."

My face felt hot with anger, and I noticed that I was clenching my fists. "You have no right to get mad at me for this. You don't have any control over my dating life."

"I guess I thought that maybe since we went on a date that that would mean something, but I guess I was wrong."

"Was that a date? It's not like you called it that."

Eli scoffed, but he recoiled as if I had slapped him across the face. "Oh come on, April, you're not that dumb."

I turned around, just for a moment, because I didn't know how to respond to that without saying something I would regret. My head was pounding with a headache provoked by frustration. When I turned around to face Eli, he had his arms folded, and he looked angrier than I had ever seen him.

"I tried to kiss you at Starbucks, and you totally rejected me."

"You rejected me first!"

I rolled my eyes. "What are we, twelve?"

"You did. I took you on a date and tried to kiss you, and you made it clear you didn't want that, so I backed off. How else was I supposed to react then?"

"Maybe I changed my mind," I said, my voice suddenly quiet. Had I changed my mind?

"Clearly not if you're going out with Ryan."

I rested my hands on my hips. "You're never going to get over that, are you? You're just going to be mad forever that I went on a date with Ryan."

"I just can't take the whiplash. You're sending a lot of mixed signals, you know."

"Oh, *I'm* the one sending mixed signals? I'm not the one who showed up again after all these years and tried to pick up like nothing ever happened between us."

Surprisingly, Eli furrowed his eyebrows, looking confused. "I don't know what you're talking about."

"We didn't speak for years, Eli. What was that? Just because I went to school in Florida, you stopped speaking to me?"

"*You* stopped speaking to *me*. You totally cut me off when we started college."

"I did not. I tried to stay in touch."

"Yeah, for like a month, and then you dropped me. I know now you were disappointed about Boston University, but April, I didn't know that then. All I knew was that my best friend completely severed all connection, and I never even knew why."

Eli had dropped his arms to his side, and he looked a little defeated, much of the anger that was just obscuring his face faded. I thought about it, and I had severed all connection with Eli. I had thought I was protecting him as well as protecting myself. I hadn't wanted to make Eli homesick. I'd thought it would be better if he didn't miss me, so I had pulled back. Plus, it had just been easier to avoid Eli rather than have to talk about why I wasn't going to Boston. It seemed so silly now, but at the time, I'd thought I was protecting him. Why was it so hard to communicate when you were a teenager? Everything felt like it had to be a secret. And why did it feel so hard to untangle the mess now?

"I thought I was helping," I finally said. "I thought maybe you'd miss home less and enjoy NYU more if I wasn't hanging around."

"Oh please, you did it for yourself. You didn't want to admit you weren't going."

That one hurt. "That's unfair."

"Is it? It apparently took you ten years to tell your best friend what happened."

"I was afraid you would make me feel bad about it. So glad I was wrong," I said, and I didn't bother to hide the sarcastic bite that laced my words.

"Hey, I tried to apologize the other day, but you didn't give me a chance. I was blindsided by everything."

"What do you mean 'everything'?" And what was he trying to apologize for?

"I tried to apologize because I felt bad for not being a good enough friend to know that you were struggling, and I always felt bad that I didn't reach out after your dad's accident, but we already hadn't spoken in years. I thought you wouldn't want to hear from me. But after you told me what happened, I felt bad, so I wanted to say something, but then you seemed like—I don't know—"

"Like I wanted to kiss you."

He nodded, but his jaw clenched. "But how was I supposed to respond to that when you had rejected me days before?"

"It felt wrong to kiss you then."

"Gee, thanks."

I folded my arms. "Because I knew I hadn't been totally honest with you and because I knew Ryan wanted to get together when he got to town."

"Ryan had *already* asked you out?"

Wrong answer.

"I didn't want to lead you on."

"All you've done is lead me on. I've been pretty clear, haven't I? I took you on a date, I offered to help with the reunion, I danced with you. I showed you my parents' house and asked for your opinion, for goodness' sake."

"Yeah, and as far as I knew, all of that was normal friend stuff. And you're the one who pulled back that day at Starbucks."

"Because you said you might still want to move to Boston," he said, and that gave me pause. Had I said that? I remembered thinking that I was liking the idea of staying in River Glen. Maybe I hadn't been as committed to that as I had thought. "You know I want to stay here, and when you said you were still thinking of Boston, I figured we didn't stand a chance. So yeah, I backed off. What else was I supposed to do?"

And that was the problem, wasn't it? What else were we supposed to do with this?

"I didn't say I was moving to Boston," I said, and it felt like a stupid thing to say. What did it matter?

"You didn't say you weren't," Eli said so quietly that it was more shocking that the yelling we'd both done standing in this alley. Eli and I were never quiet. We were arguing playfully or laughing or apparently even fighting, but we were never quiet. It felt so alien that it hurt more than the accusations we'd hurled at each other.

"Look," he finally said after a long silence, "pick whichever reunion games you and Ryan want, and go on a date if you really want to. I don't care anymore."

I watched him grab his stuff from inside and walk away, and it hurt far more than it had hurt the other day or than it had ten years ago. I felt like I was watching Eli walk away from me forever.

CLASS OF 2014

Most Likely to
Become President

EMMA WILSON

Most Likely to
Marry First

QUINN PENDLETON

Most Likely to Move
Back to River Glen

ELI FORRESTER

Most Likely to Drop
Out of College

DANNY LINK

Class Clown

TRACE PECK

Most Likely to
Become Famous

QUINN PENDLETON

Best Smile

PAIGE SOMERVILLE

Most School Spirit

EMMA WILSON

Most Athletic

RYAN BENNINGS

Most Likely to
Succeed

APRIL CORWIN

14

I had spent most of the weekend holed up in my apartment working on my thesis. For months, I had found any excuse to distract
myself from working on it because I felt such a lack of confidence in
my abilities to finish the darn thing. Now, it was my excuse to distract
myself from thinking about anything else.

I'd made the edits that my thesis director had suggested, and I'd
also made some additions of my own. It was coming together in a
way that made me really excited. This was the feeling I had always
had in college. It was the feeling that had made me want to be a
professor and do this kind of research full-time. When I started this
degree coursework a couple of years ago, I had struggled to get back
into that kind of mindset. I was disappointed in how I had gotten to
this path, and I battled some pretty intense impostor syndrome. Now,
none of that really mattered anymore. What mattered was that I had
found a project idea I loved and had developed it into something really
exciting.

Now it was done. I was doing the finishing touches of formatting,
final citations, and little grammatical things, but I was finally done
writing it—all sixty-three pages of it. It had ended up being longer
than I had originally planned, but that was the way with all aspects
of my life, it seemed. It had taken me longer to get to graduate school,

longer to find joy in my job, and longer to realize what my heart really wanted.

I finished typing, emailed it to my director, and shut my laptop. Assuming he signed off on it—and I had no reason to think he wouldn't—all that was left was the defense which would probably be scheduled for November, and the defense was the least intimidating part of this after working at it for so long. I had finally made it.

But there was a hollowness to this accomplishment. Had I finally realized what I wanted too late? How much time had I wasted hating my life over the past few years? What else could I have gotten out of my time at FSU if I hadn't spent so much of it bitter that it wasn't BU? How much better of a teacher could I have been if I hadn't spent so long thinking of it as a temporary job and not a career?

What would Eli and I be now if I hadn't pushed him away?

My education and my job were fixable things—honestly, they were things that maybe weren't even broken to begin with. Education and work skills were things that grew over time, not things that were ever truly complete. I had to change that mindset.

But I didn't think relationships worked exactly the same way. Sure, there was a growth element to relationships, but they did feel like the kind of thing that could be broken, could be missed entirely. I might have irreparably damaged my relationship with Eli, and I didn't know what to do about that. I wasn't sure anything could be done.

But I also couldn't help but wonder if Eli and I had tried to force something that just wasn't meant to be. Maybe we were better off as friends, and the problems started because we tried to be something we just weren't. I had a date with Ryan this week, and Ryan was everything I was looking for in a guy. I was so looking forward to our date.

But then why did I weirdly feel like going on a date with Ryan was some kind of betrayal of Eli?

I shook my head and grabbed the remote and flicked the TV on. I had to distract myself. This was what came of not being busy enough. When I had to focus on grading papers, planning a reunion, and finishing my thesis, I didn't have time to worry about my romantic life. It was easier that way, but it wasn't necessarily better.

I grabbed my senior yearbook and absent-mindedly flipped through it until I hit the senior superlative page. I had been voted the "Most Likely to Succeed" award. At the time, I had thought that I had only won that one because everyone either couldn't think of someone else to give that to or couldn't think of anything else to give me. It was so generic and nonspecific. What did "success" mean to a bunch of high school seniors, and why had they thought I was likely to achieve it? I glanced at some of the others, and while many had been pretty accurate then and still remained so, others were laughable. This was the kind of thing you looked back on as an adult and laughed because your teenage self was so foolish. I'd had a pretty clear idea of what success was back then, and if I was still using that rubric, then I had failed. But I wasn't using that rubric anymore. Honestly, I wasn't using any rubric anymore. I was done judging myself based on made up standards in my own head. My class had been right: I was successful.

I glanced over at the superlative game Ryan had suggested. It was a game to guess which of the superlatives had come true, and whoever guessed the most correct won a gift card. It was a cute idea, but how would we define whether or not these were true now? Would my classmates consider me successful? Was Ryan still most athletic? Did Paige still have the best smile? It was all so subjective. I supposed it always was, but in high school it had seemed there were right and wrong answers to these kinds of questions. Now I didn't know how to quantify these things.

One thing was for sure: Eli had been voted most likely to move back to River Glen, and that was happening just in time for his superlative to be true. That was the way with Eli—everything was clear cut.

Thinking about Eli still caused a stinging feeling. I hated some of the things I had said to him as much as I hated some of the things he had said to me. Still, I wanted him in my life. I wanted to make amends, however that would look. And I didn't know how that would fit in with a date with Ryan.

Ryan. I wondered about him, too. I had always wanted a date with him, and now I had it. He was living my dream life in Boston. I was getting way ahead of myself, but what was stopping me from moving to Boston and teaching high school there? I knew the answer, of course: my students. I'd grown attached to them, but that felt silly. I taught juniors and seniors. In two years, they would all graduate anyway. Besides, wouldn't I get attached to any students I taught? Couldn't I love new students somewhere else as much as I loved my current ones? But something felt wrong about that, too. Why could I not picture myself teaching anywhere but River Glen Academy anymore?

In some ways, my life felt like it had so much clarity now, but in other ways, it was more confusing than ever.

Dear Diary~*~

This is maybe the most cliche thing I've ever written, but why do guys like Ryan Bennings never notice girls like me? It's like there's some kind of external force in high school that pushes the football players toward the cheerleaders, the theater kids toward each other, and girls like me toward — well, no one.

I don't think any guy at River Glen has ever liked me. And Ryan is so nice and such a good guy, and he always talks to me in the hallways or in class, but it's never more than that. I guess he's just destined to be that guy from high school that I always look back on and think "what if?" It's not like Ryan is ever going to see me as a girl he wants to date.

~*~April

15

— · —

Ryan told me he booked the Silver Swan Bar & Grill for dinner, and that in and of itself made me anxious. It was a nicer restaurant than I was used to going to. Nothing wildly fancy or anything—this was River Glen after all—but it wasn't the diner down the road or the local chain restaurant. How should one dress for a date to the Silver Swan? How should one dress for a date with Ryan Bennings?

I had managed to narrow down my choices to two dresses, and that was a feat. I was torn between a golden yellow dress and a blush pink dress. The yellow dress was knee-length, A-line, and sleeveless with a square neckline. I liked the way the fabric swished when I walked. It was one of my favorite dresses, and I wore it all the time. The pink dress was an impulse buy while shopping at the outlet mall last year. I couldn't have afforded it anywhere but at the outlets, but I had desperately wanted something nicer to wear when the occasion arose. Of course, it never had because I was a teacher, and the nicest event I could expect to attend was prom. It was a little more fitted, also sleeveless, with a sweetheart neckline. I pretty much never wore it. It felt too nice for work—and honestly, a little too tight for being a teacher—but maybe that meant this was the perfect time to wear it? Hadn't I bought it while dreaming of dating someone exactly like

Ryan who would invite me to fancy dinners? But when I stepped in front of the mirror and saw how I looked in the yellow dress, I remembered why it was my favorite.

I grabbed my phone and video called Paige. She didn't answer, so I immediately called her a second time. Being a best friend meant answering frantic video messages on a Saturday night. How could she think otherwise?

Paige finally answered, not bothering to hide the annoyance in her voice. "What?" she said around a mouthful of popcorn. "I'm in the middle of a *CSI* marathon."

"When are you not in the middle of a *CSI* marathon? I need your help." I propped the phone up on my dresser and stepped back. "Yellow dress?" I held up the hanger with the pink dress on it. "Or pink dress."

"Pink dress for sure," she said.

"Really?"

She nodded. "Definitely. The yellow dress looks like a teacher dress."

"Uh, in case you haven't noticed, I am a teacher."

"Yeah, but your dress shouldn't scream 'teacher' on a date with a handsome accountant. The pink is prettier. More date-like."

"If you say so." I slipped the yellow dress off and shimmied into the pink one. I looked in the mirror and silently admitted that it did look good. I grabbed a simple cubic zirconia necklace and clipped it before stepping back into frame.

"See?" Paige said. "It's perfect. Don't forget earrings."

I grabbed a pair of studs. "Nude or black heels?"

"Nude."

I was hoping she would say that. My black heels were uncomfortable. I only wore them when I had to, like to the annual Christmas choral performance or to local theater productions.

"When is he picking you up?"

I checked my watch. "Any minute. How do I look?"

Paige mimed a chef's kiss. "Perfect. Call me after and tell me everything."

I flitted my hand at her. "I'll call you tomorrow."

"Oooh, planning on a late night, are we?" she wiggled her eyebrows.

"I'm hanging up now."

"Don't kiss on the first date!"

I hung up before she could rattle off anything else. I shoved my phone in my clutch, stepped into the heels, and started for the door. I stopped only for a moment to look back at the yellow dress strewn across my bed. I thought about making a last minute switch, but when I heard my doorbell ring, I gave up the thought. I was being silly. This was the right dress for a date night, and I finally had an excuse to wear it.

***

At the restaurant, Ryan held the door for me and told his name to the hostess who turned to grab some menus. I hadn't been to the Silver Swan in a long time. It looked the same and yet totally different all at the same time. The owners must have done some remodeling recently, but the changes were minor: some new paint, maybe reupholstered chairs. Otherwise, it looked the same as the last time I'd been there which was years ago at this point. In fact, I thought the last time I was here was when my parents had taken me here to celebrate my getting the job at River Glen Academy. At the time, I hadn't exactly felt like celebrating. Getting the job at River Glen back then had felt like confirmation that I was stuck in River Glen forever. I didn't really feel that way anymore.

The hostess handed some menus to the other hostess next to her and pointed to us. The second hostess took them, but when her eyes met mine, she smiled wide and squealed.

"Ms. Corwin!"

"Ellie," I said, "good to see you. I didn't know you worked here."

She nodded. "For about six months now. I can take you and your, uh, friend to your table."

I touched Ryan's arm. "Ryan, this is one of my students. Ellie, this is Ryan. We graduated together, and we're planning our ten year reunion."

We followed Ellie as she talked. "Wow, ten years? Sometimes it feels like I'll never graduate, but ten years *after* graduation? That's wild to think about."

"It comes faster than you think."

"That's for sure," Ryan added.

Ellie set the menus down on a table and gestured. "Well, here we are. Your server will be Jackson. Have fun planning your reunion! And Ms. Corwin, I promise I will have that paper done on Monday. I don't have work tomorrow, so I'm going to knock the whole thing out, I swear."

I smiled. "I have no doubt, Ellie. I'll see you on Monday."

She eyed Ryan and I suspiciously, but thankfully, Ryan didn't notice. She smiled and skipped off.

Ryan looked up with a laugh from his menu. "Does that happen often?"

"What?"

He gestured in the direction in which Ellie had walked off. "That. Running into students."

Now, I laughed. "Pretty much all the time. River Glen's a small place, you know that."

"I guess I never thought about it. Is it annoying to run into students everywhere you go?"

"I used to think so. When I first started teaching, it drove me insane. I guess I've just gotten used to it now. Besides, students like Ellie I never mind."

Or really any of them, I thought. I didn't mind running into any of them: the cheerleaders, the football players, the class clowns, the grade grinders, the chatty back-of-the-class types. I liked seeing them. I couldn't really remember exactly when that had changed, but there was no denying the fact that seeing Ellie did not annoy me or make me anxious at all—it only made me smile.

"It's like you never really left high school," Ryan said.

"I mean, I'm not a student anymore. That makes a huge difference."

He laughed, and I couldn't help but admire the way he looked when he laughed. It was a natural, genuine laugh that made his face light up. "Well, no. I don't know if I could do it. High school was great, but would I want to relive it every day as my job? Probably not."

People said that to me all the time. The old "I could never do it" speech. I always wanted to explain to people that that was all careers everywhere. We all liked different things, we all had different skills. Why did people expect to like every job they heard about?

"Believe it or not," I said, "high school is *much* easier as a teacher than as a student."

"How so?"

"You just see things differently, I guess. Problems that seemed so massive and unsolvable in high school seem much simpler on this side of things. That's part of what I like about teaching, actually. I like getting to help my kids think through decisions."

Ryan raised an eyebrow. "Kids?"

I let out a nervous chuckle. "Sorry, teacher habit. We all call our students our kids."

He stretched his arm across the table and held out his hand, so I hesitantly took it. I liked the feeling of warmth it gave me to hold his hand, but it was hard to suppress the memory of Eli holding my hand when we had danced. My hand fit in his perfectly. Ryan's hand seemed too big for mine. "That's sweet."

I smiled, but we seemed stuck for more conversation. Now we were just holding hands across the table, and while I certainly didn't mind if that continued, the longer that the silence stretched on, the more awkward it became.

"So," I said, desperate to find something to talk about, "tell me more about your job. I feel like I don't really know what you do."

He laughed. "Our firm handles accounting services for businesses." When he didn't continue, I raised an eyebrow, and he smiled. "Basically, we do payroll, financial planning, investing, and other services for businesses. We have mostly smaller businesses, but we've gained some pretty big accounts lately, so that's good."

"And what do you do specifically?"

"I'm mostly involved in the new business services. We help businesses get started with all of that paperwork, financial stuff, and so on. I work with a team that then does the financial planning side."

"That sounds like a lot of pressure."

"How so?" he asked.

"It feels like it's a lot of responsibility to help a new business get started. I remember when Paige started the Donutisserie, she was so stressed out keeping track of everything." It wasn't a responsibility I ever wanted to have. I was perfectly happy to work at an established place like a school and let someone else handle the business management side.

"That's actually what I like about the job," he said. "I do this kind of stuff all day, so it's easy for me. I get a chance to ease some of the stress new business owners have."

That made sense. I guessed if it was something you did all day, it wouldn't be hard.

He continued, "Plus, it's kind of a fun part of the job. So much of business is building relationships. Our firm is trusted, and our clients recommend us to their friends or associates. I'm out of the office multiple times of the week having business lunches or visiting office spaces. I never pictured myself in a suit making deals over lunch in a nice restaurant, but I guess that's adulthood."

Our waiter came over and took our orders, and I ordered the chicken piccata after much internal debate. I wasn't as used to restaurants like this as Ryan was. I would much rather eat a cheeseburger at a diner than a place like this, but I decided eating a burger would not look very ladylike, and chicken was hard to mess up, right?

Ryan ordered a cut of steak I'd never heard of as well as some kind of shrimp appetizer. I wondered what it was like to eat at fancy restaurants twice a week, but I couldn't imagine it was relaxing. Ryan wasn't just enjoying a meal—he was expected to make a successful business deal, score a client. The thought flitted through my head, and I suppressed it before I could fully grasp hold of it: were dates just another kind of business client? Was I a "client" to score?

"Plus," Ryan said as if he hadn't been interrupted by the waiter, "the food in Boston is amazing. I swear, every restaurant I've gone to is incredible."

"Oh, I know. I think that's my favorite part of Boston. Other than the history, obviously."

"I wish I could say I've seen more of the historical sites, but honestly, I can't ever find the time. But I've definitely made my way around the food circuit," he said with a chuckle. I knew I was a history teacher, so obviously I had a bigger interest in American history than most, but how could someone live in the heart of American history and not care?

"Don't you ever repeat restaurants?" I had this image in my mind of Ryan having a reserved table at a specific restaurant—something like the Silver Swan—that he waltzes in and claims every Thursday at noon. I wasn't sure where I got that picture in my head, but now that it was there, I couldn't get it out. It sounded so stressful to me to try to decide on a new meal all the time while simultaneously trying to do my job.

"Of course I do, but I try not to get stuck in a rut at the same place all the time. Every place has great food. That's one of the things I love about Boston. I never have to go to the same places, see the same people. Every day is something different, so I never get bored. You know how it is." He gestured around him. "In River Glen, you see the same people every day at the same places. It gets kind of monotonous."

I nodded as our food arrived, but my thoughts drifted while Ryan told me about a specific restaurant he'd gone to last month. It *was* the same thing every day around here, and a few years ago, I might have agreed with Ryan's assessment of it as being monotonous, but the word that came to my mind now was consistent. I liked the consistency of River Glen. I knew that Paige always made the s'mores donuts on Fridays and that the coffee shop by my parents' house opened two hours later on Sundays because the older woman who owned it never missed a church service. Every Friday night, the whole town would show up for a football game at River Glen Academy, and we almost always lost, but no one cared. I knew that I was always welcome at my parents' for dinner unless it was Wednesday night because my mom had book club. Every other Saturday, there was a farmer's market downtown, and every Christmas, kids would line up in the park to meet Santa while it rained fake snow made out of soap bubbles. River Glen was predictable, and I didn't think it was a bad thing anymore.

"Boston's just such a cool place, you know?" Ryan said, and I realized I had zoned out for a while. I didn't even know what he was talking about anymore. I just nodded and agreed and hoped he wouldn't notice I hadn't been listening. "I just love how big it is. There's always a new restaurant to try or a new coffee shop to hit or a new client to meet. I never see the same person twice."

I was struck by how much that didn't sound like a positive thing to me. I liked seeing Paige every day and running into my students when I was out. I liked living so close to my parents and running into all their friends who still called me "young lady." Pretty much every local business was owned by someone I'd known my whole life.

In fact, the only time I'd ever lived anywhere else was college, and looking back now, I remembered feeling so homesick. FSU was so big, and even though I made really great friends there, it was always so much effort to get together. We had to plan to see each other—there was no chance of just bumping into each other. I had felt really isolated there. At the time, I had thought that it was because FSU wasn't my first choice, but in hindsight, maybe that wasn't the problem at all.

"That doesn't get lonely?" I asked.

"Not at all," he said. "It's exciting. It's a new adventure every day. I mean, River Glen was a cool place to grow up and all, but I wouldn't trade my life in Boston for anything. I'm living the dream. I have a good job, a nice place, and I get to visit all these cool places every week."

Ryan smiled, and it was genuine. He really did love his life in Boston, and I was so happy for him. But I couldn't get Eli's words out of my head. He'd left New York because he couldn't picture his life there long-term. He didn't like how impersonal it was. He wanted to build relationships with his patients and raise a family in River Glen. When I looked back on my own childhood, it was hard to argue with that logic. I'd had a good childhood. I'd made lifelong friends like Eli and Paige; I'd been loved, protected, and encouraged by the people in this town; I'd been bolstered by people who had always believed in me even when I hadn't believed in myself; I'd even had support in the aftermath of my dad's car accident. Would any of that have been true if I'd grown up in a city? Maybe, but could I imagine it?

I wanted to raise a family in a place like River Glen, too. No, not a place like River Glen. Just River Glen. I didn't think I'd really known that until Eli said it, and then I couldn't shake the thought. He'd gone and lived the dream we both thought we had, and he'd found it wanting and come back. I never left, but maybe I didn't need to. Maybe I was happy here and just needed to accept it finally. Maybe I needed to stop fighting it because of some weird idea I'd gotten in my head that staying in a small town like River Glen meant failure.

I set my fork down and watched Ryan. He was telling me about a business party he'd attended. His enthusiasm shone from his eyes as he talked. He really did love the schmoozing and the business and the city life. For the first time, I couldn't picture myself there. I didn't see myself drinking wine or champagne in a stuffy restaurant in a dress like the one I was currently wearing. I didn't see myself walking down the streets of Boston or taking a train and not seeing one face I knew. I pictured myself here in my classroom staring at the faces of my kids. I saw myself at a family dinner on Sunday nights in a pretty craftsman house, not a high-rise apartment building. I pictured myself at the Donutisserie with Paige. I pictured myself playing Scrabble at the family dinner night I was currently skipping to be here.

And I pictured myself with Eli, not Ryan.

I realized I'd been staring at my plate, and when I looked up, I found that Ryan had noticed, too. He smiled, but his eyebrows remained furrowed. "Are you okay?" he asked.

"Yes, I'm fine, sorry."

He laughed lightly. "That's my bad. I'm droning on and on about business on a date."

"No, Ryan, you're not wrong. I love how happy your job makes you. I'm so glad you love it and Boston, but I just realized something."

"What's that?"

"I always pictured myself in Boston or a place like it. In high school, I couldn't wait to get out of here and go anywhere else."

"But you don't feel that way anymore." He said it as a statement not a question.

"How did you—"

"I might not be good at making conversation on a date, but I'm not totally clueless." He smiled, set his silverware down, and reached out his hand. I took it, but it didn't feel the same anymore. He looked down at our hands, and I could tell he felt it, too. "I can tell you're really happy here. You absolutely lit up when you saw your student, and you light up every time you talk about them."

I nodded. "I really do love them. I didn't think I would love teaching high school, but it's perfect. I just don't think I can picture myself anywhere but River Glen anymore."

He squeezed my hand gently before letting it go. "I guess I missed my chance, then. That's what I get for waiting ten years to ask a girl out."

I let a small laugh escape my lips. "Ryan, you're a wonderful guy. I've always known that. You were great in high school, and you still are, but you deserve to be with someone who loves the same life you do. I just don't think I'm her." *Not anymore*, I thought. But then, maybe I never was. Maybe I was in love with an idea of a life and a version of myself I thought I could be. I didn't want that anymore, and I realized that that was all Ryan ever was to me also: an idea.

"But I'm so glad we had this time together now," I added, and it was true. I finally got the date with Ryan Bennings, and it was everything I thought it would be. It just wasn't right for me, and I was finally okay with that. "And I can't wait for the rest of our class to see what we came up with for the reunion."

He smiled, and even though there was a touch of sadness to it, he sounded sincere when he said, "I know it'll be fantastic. You did a great job, Corwin. You always do."

Eli~

I never explained what happened, why I chose FSU over BU, and I thought you deserved an explanation.

I didn't get the financial aid I needed to go to Boston, and after my grandfather's death a few months ago, I just couldn't leave home. I wish I were in Boston right now and that you and I were spending weekends exploring Boston and New York City like we planned, but I just couldn't do it. I didn't want to tell you because I feel like such a failure, and I didn't want you to feel bad for me or feel like you were alone. I guess you kind of are alone now, and I hate that, but I know that you'll be all right. You always are.

I don't know why it felt harder to tell you what happened than it felt with everyone else. You just mean more, I guess. You always have. I had kind of pictured life long-term with you in the Northeast, and I didn't know how to let go of that. Somehow, telling you would have made it more real, and I don't want to make it real. I don't want to picture life without you.

I hope that you love New York and that NYU is everything you wanted it to be and more. I hope you can forgive me for not going up there and not telling you about it. I would hate it if I lost your friendship. I would hate it if I lost you.

Maybe I'll get to be up there for grad school, and we can earn Master's degrees together. I hope so.

~April

16

Friday night, I parked in the staff parking lot and started the walk over to the football field. It was a long walk from the staff parking lot which was on the opposite side of campus, but tonight, I didn't mind. I considered grabbing a hat from my back seat, but the weather was actually not too bad tonight, so I decided to leave my hair down. I wore black joggers and a blue RGA staff shirt. I owned so many of those staff shirts that it felt like they were taking over my wardrobe, but now I liked them.

As I walked over to the football field, I thought about how crazy tonight was. Ten years ago, I would have been attending the homecoming football game as a high school senior. I'd been the newspaper editor, and I'd had good grades in rigorous classes. I'd had plans to go to Boston University and become a history professor. I'd had such a clear plan for my life. My life hadn't turned out anything like I thought it would, but I wasn't unhappy. In fact, I was pretty happy with how it had turned out. I liked my job, I liked Model UN, I liked being close to my parents, and I liked how my thesis had turned out. I hadn't known how much of a drastic difference ten years could make, but I no longer feared what could happen in ten years. I wasn't disappointed anymore, and I looked forward to what life would look like in River Glen for the next ten years.

The only part of the future that made my heart ache was that I feared that Eli wouldn't be a part of it anymore. Just when I realized that maybe we did want the same things after all, I pushed him away without meaning to and then meaning to. That was one of the hardest parts of growing up, I thought. It was so hard to understand when your desires and goals for the future just changed. It didn't mean the old desires and goals were bad or even that the new ones were better; it just meant that I wasn't the same person at twenty-eight as I had been at eighteen, and that was okay. It was normal. But part of wanting different things at twenty-eight was wanting a different kind of man. Ryan had seemed like he was the perfect man, and I was certain that he would be for some other girl, a girl who wanted to live in a city and go to a new restaurant every weekend and work a successful desk job in business. I just wasn't that girl anymore. Part of me wondered if maybe I never was. It didn't matter anymore.

What did matter was that the only person I wanted to see tonight was Eli. Paige wasn't coming—she was baking a batch of donuts to be ready for the Saturday rush—and Ryan and I had already made our peace. Quinn certainly didn't want to see me, and Emma wasn't coming. Sure, I had other friends in my class, and there were people I would enjoy seeing, but I felt like none of it mattered if I didn't see Eli tonight. I had no idea if he was even coming. Surely he would come despite our fight, right? He had friends he probably wanted to see. Still, I didn't see his rental car in the parking lot, and that made my spirit drop a little.

When I entered the gate to the bleacher seating, the cheerleaders waved excitedly, shouting a chorus of, "Ms. Corwin!" I smiled and waved. It was so sweet to see students who were so excited to see me. I had worked really hard to build a good rapport with my students. I remembered the teachers I'd had who had gone out of their way to be kind and let students know that they actually cared, and I had tried really hard to be that teacher.

I turned the corner, and just past the concessions stand, I could see the banquet hall that we used for special events filled with my classmates. This was kind of the soft start into the reunion. The actual reunion was tomorrow in the park, but some people liked to come to the homecoming football game. I glanced inside and saw a decent attendance, but I knew—or at least hoped—that a lot more would come tomorrow. Not everyone cared about a high school football game once they weren't in high school.

But I did. I cared about high school football. In some ways, I cared more than I had as a student. As a student, football games had been social activities, and I hardly watched the game. As a teacher, I loved going to my students' athletic events. My students who were football players would ask me every Friday during class if I was coming to the game, and it was so hard to say no when they looked at you so earnestly hoping that their U.S. history teacher would go to their game. How could I say no? And when I saw them score a touchdown or force another down or pull off an impressive pass or tackle, it was so much fun to tell them on Monday at school and see them light up. I loved when the cheerleaders waved to me while cheering on the sidelines. I loved seeing random students walk by socializing with their friends but stopping to say hi to me—even if it was just to ask for an extension on an assignment.

Before I could head toward the banquet hall, a group of girls waved and ran over to me. It was Ellie, Katie, and Anna, all of whom were in my AP U.S. history class, and they were followed closely by a couple of seniors, Jorie and Wesley, who were in my one section of American government.

"Ms. Corwin!" Ellie said. "You came."

"I told you I would," I said. "I never miss the homecoming game."

"The game just started," Wesley said. "Nothing's really happened yet."

"Oh good, I'm glad I didn't miss anything."

"Dennis is starting tonight," Anna said.

Katie added, "First time he's started this year. He's so excited."

"That's great," I said.

"We're about to sit down," Jorie said. "Come sit with us, Ms. Corwin."

"Oh, you're sweet, but I was actually headed over there—"

I stopped myself. I was about to say that I was headed into the banquet hall for the reunion, but why? I peeked inside, and I still didn't see Eli. I thought about going in there, and what was the point? The people I wanted to see I would see tomorrow at the actual reunion. Would sitting in there just mean sitting by myself in a corner wishing Eli were there? I looked at the five students standing in front of me, and I made a decision that probably would have surprised me ten years ago.

"Actually, sure," I said. "As long as you don't think it's uncool to sit with your teacher."

They all laughed. "Oh my gosh, no, Ms. Corwin," Katie said. "You're a cool teacher."

"Seriously," Jorie added. "Come on. There's a whole group already over in the student section."

I followed them and practically laughed out loud at the irony. I'd never sat in the student section when I was in high school. Maybe I'd thought I wasn't cool enough or maybe I just didn't really care back then, but now I was about to sit in the student section with at least twenty of my students who were waving and cheering as they saw me approach with the others. And I was so happy to join them.

I used to think teaching was the kind of job that was mobile, that I could do anywhere, and that was still more or less true. High school teaching jobs were everywhere, and I could find students I would care about anywhere. But *these* students weren't everywhere—they were right here, and that was where I wanted to be.

***

As the football game was winding down, I decided to slip out before everyone else to avoid the traffic glut that always happened at the end of games. I slipped out a side entrance that Eli and I had always used to use in high school to avoid the crowds. It was under the bleachers, and nobody except students really used it. I didn't think the parents even knew about it. Even though Eli and I always went out this way back then, I didn't expect to see him there tonight.

"Oh, hey," I said.

"Hey," he said. "I didn't see you in the banquet hall."

"I didn't go."

"Oh."

"I was planning to, but I ran into some students, and they wanted me to sit with them."

He cracked a tiny smile. "That's sweet."

"I'm still going tomorrow, though," I quickly added then felt dumb for doing so. I had planned the whole thing, so why wouldn't I go? I just hated the silence, I guess.

"I'm glad."

Everything about Eli was totally unreadable, and I hated that. Eli and I were always so attuned to each other. It wasn't until after we lost touch that this distance crept in between us. I had noticed it when he first got to town, and I felt like we had finally overcome it. Now, it was back, and it was my fault. I had let myself get distracted by Ryan and by my own insecurities and and fears about the future. Eli hadn't deserved that, not ten years ago, and not now.

But we weren't in high school anymore, not eighteen years old anymore. I wasn't going to make the same mistakes again even if the damage was already done.

" I just wanted to say that I'm sorry," I said. "I shouldn't have gotten mad at you over the whole Ryan thing. You were right: we weren't right for each other, and I was foolish to think that that had changed just because we were older."

He shrugged, but not in a dismissive way, more of a resigned way. "I shouldn't have gotten so angry. It's none of my business. I let an old high school grudge get the better of me."

"And I should have been honest with you ten years ago. I was just so embarrassed, and I felt like I had failed, and I didn't want to admit that to you."

"Even me?"

"Especially you. You matter to me, Eli. You always have. I just didn't realize how much."

"Well—"

"I wrote you a letter back then, you know," I said, cutting him off. "I wrote an email explaining what happened and why I didn't go to Boston University."

He furrowed his eyebrows. "I never got an email."

I smiled, void of joy. "I never sent it. It just sat in my drafts folder. I chickened out of sending it because I was scared. I was scared to tell you everything because I thought you might pity me or not want to go to NYU, and I know how stupid that sounds. Of course you had to go to NYU, and don't think that I thought you would change all your plans for me or anything, but, I don't know, I guess when you're eighteen, you don't always see things clearly. I think that was also the first time I realized how much I cared about you, and I was scared to allow that realization. I didn't know what it meant to admit that I liked my best friend, so I didn't admit it." I stopped to pull an envelope from my crossbody leather bag. "I printed the email, and I know that's so dumb because I could have just sent it, but I guess I wanted to hand this to you old-school style."

Eli took it hesitatingly. "You printed it?"

I nodded. "Obviously there's not really a point to it anymore. You know everything now, and I don't know if it would have even made a difference back then or not, but regardless of where we stand now, I want you to know that I still care about you a lot. I always did. That never stopped. And I'm not moving to Boston or dating Ryan or any of that. I'm done living for some imagined life that I've put on a weird pedestal in my mind. I want to continue teaching here at RGA, and I want to have dinner with my parents every Thursday night. I'm happy here, and I can finally accept that. I really want you to be a part of my life here, and I hope you can accept my apology and that we can be friends even if we can't be more than that."

Eli opened his mouth like he wanted to say something, but he seemed to struggle to find the words, so I spoke again. "I'm so proud of you for becoming an orthodontist, and I hope you can make your old house your new house and that it'll be everything you want it to be. I'll see you tomorrow."

I walked away before Eli had a chance to respond and before I had a chance to say something I would regret. I'd always loved him as a friend, and it had always seemed like that was all we would ever be, and that was okay. Eli and I had been comfortable together. It never used to feel weird to think of loving Eli—at least, not until that love became something more than platonic. Somewhere along the line, I had started to think of Eli in romantic terms, and I hadn't realized it until now.

The truth was that I loved Eli Forrester, and I realized I might have been too late.

CLASS OF 2014
TEN YEAR REUNION PLAYLIST

►	Shake It Off	Taylor Swift	3:39
►	Bartender	Lady A	3:18
►	Maps	Maroon 5	3:09
►	Happy	Pharrell Williams	3:52
►	All of Me	John Legend	4:29
►	Counting Stars	OneRepublic	4:17
►	Pompeii	Bastille	3:34
►	Am I Wrong	Nico & Vinz	4:05
►	Wake Me Up	Avicii	4:07
►	Radioactive	Imagine Dragons	3:06
►	Story of My Life	One Direction	4:05
►	Chandelier	Sia	3:36
►	Royals	Lorde	3:10
►	Boom Clap	Charli XCX	2:49
►	Roar	Katy Perry	3:43
►	Ain't It Fun	Paramore	4:56
►	Classic	MKTO	2:55
►	Play It Again	Luke Bryan	3:46
►	Love Runs Out	OneRepublic	3:44
►	Me and My Broken Heart	Rixton	3:13
►	Brave	Sara Bareilles	3:40

01:10 ———————●——————————— 04:10

⟲   ◄◄   ❚❚   ►►   ⤮

17

The night of the reunion, I didn't have nearly as much trouble choosing an outfit as I had for my date with Ryan. That night, I'd still been trying to be someone I thought I wanted to be, someone I thought I could be. I wasn't doing that anymore. I wasn't going to make efforts to hide the fact that I was a teacher in a small town and loved it. I was proud of who I was, and I just wasn't content to hide anything about myself. So I grabbed the yellow dress, my favorite dress, that I had discarded the night of my date with Ryan. It was the wrong dress to wear on a date with a high-powered businessman who lived in the city. But I wasn't the kind of girl who wanted to date a man like that. Not anymore. I hoped Ryan would find the right girl for him—he really was still such a nice guy. But I wasn't going to try to convince myself that I could be her anymore. This yellow dress was the kind of dress a teacher wore to her high school reunion in a small town.

I chose not to wear a necklace—it would probably just irritate me later if it got hot. Instead, I wore some drop earrings and loosely curled my hair. The curls probably wouldn't hold all night, but that was fine with me. I thought about wearing heels, but I decided against it since we'd be in the park, so instead I wore brown wedges that had only a slight heel. I smiled when I saw myself in the mirror. I was comfortable with who I was, and I liked that I was proud of myself after all these years. My only regret was that I wished I could have shared this moment with Eli. I hoped we could still somehow work our way back to friendship even though the thought of being only friends with Eli made me feel a little sick.

***

"Excellent work, April," Mr. Quentin said as he walked over to where I was greeting classmates as they entered.

"Thank you," I answered, "but I didn't expect to see you tonight."

"Oh, I'm not staying. I just came to sign the final checks and see how everything turned out. It seems you did a marvelous job."

"I had some help from some of the other classmates."

"I don't suppose I could talk you into planning future reunions, could I?"

I laughed but smiled politely. "Sorry, Mr. Quentin, but this was a one-time deal. Although, I might be willing to plan my twenty year reunion. We'll have to see."

He smiled. "I'm glad you're thinking you'll be here long term."

"Oh, absolutely. You're not getting rid of me that easily."

"Good to know. Have a wonderful night. Enjoy your reunion."

He walked off to talk to talk to Karen, presumably to give her the last check. So far, everyone was raving about the food. I was so glad Paige had told us about Karen. Her food was definitely the hit of the night. Well, second only to the location. It was still a pretty warm night, but everyone loved the park location. It was so pretty with all the lights strung on the trees and the candle-lit tables scattered around. Dancing had been slow to start, but once a few of the more popular students from our class had started dancing, everyone else had joined in.

"Hey."

I turned around to see Ryan smiling behind me, his hands in his pockets.

"Hey," I said. "So, what do you think?"

He looked around and smiled. "Everything is perfect, April," he said, and I was surprised that he didn't call me "Corwin." "I can't thank you enough for your help. I never would have been able to pull this off from Boston. Honestly, when Emma told me she wasn't coming, I was really worried, but I'm so glad I had you to help me."

"I'm just glad everything worked out."

"And I hope that we can still be friends even if it didn't work out between us."

"Of course," I said, then gave him a hug. "Maybe Paige and I will still visit Boston, and we can all get together."

His smile widened. "Definitely. I'm going to head over and start some of the entertainment, but I just wanted to thank you again and tell you—tell you that you look really beautiful tonight. I hope Eli knows how lucky he is."

I shook my head slightly. "What?"

"Oh come on." Ryan chuckled. "I'm not clueless. I saw the way he looked at you, and I saw the way you looked back at him. I was pretty sure he had a thing for you back in high school, but we're not in high school anymore, and he's obviously still into you."

Ryan's words made me happy and sad at the same time. At once, he was confirming everything I hoped was true but also what might be lost forever. Ryan didn't know about the fight between me and Eli. A not-so-tiny part of me hoped that maybe Ryan was right and that whatever he had seen between us could transcend that, but I wasn't sure.

"No, I guess we're not in high school anymore," I said, and I wasn't even sure what I meant. Ryan had meant it as an encouragement, that we were adults now who could admit when we had feelings and pursue them. But maybe I meant that the past was the past, and maybe it couldn't be relived.

"There he is now," Ryan said, nodding his head in the direction behind me. I whipped my head around to see Eli approaching. He was wearing dark wash jeans and a gray button down shirt with the sleeves rolled up. He looked so good that it hurt, and I noticed he was snapping his fingers again. "I'll leave you to it," Ryan said as he walked away.

I waved to Eli, unsure if he would come over to talk to me, but he waved back and headed over. I didn't know what he would say. Was he still angry? Did he want to be friends? I knew what I wanted him to say, but I wasn't sure I could hope for that, so I found myself trying to decide what the second-best option was.

"Hey," I said, smiling and trying to seem normal.

He smiled, too. "It looks like it's going well."

I nodded. "Everyone loves the food, and it seems like everyone is happy with the park venue even though it's a little warm. Well, everyone except Quinn."

He laughed, and it seemed more genuine than the smile had seemed. "If Quinn is the only person who's unhappy, then I think this is a smash. Do you think we could talk for a minute?"

It was coming: whatever Eli was going to say was coming, and I didn't know how to prepare. I nodded at my coworker who was manning the check-in table with me and walked toward a quiet part of the park with Eli.

He pulled my printed email out of his pocket and smirked. "So I read this, and I still think it's kind of funny that you printed a ten-year-old email for me."

I shrugged. "I didn't know what else to do. I don't know, maybe I should have just deleted it and never told you about it all. It's so pointless all these years later. I just felt like—I don't know, I guess I just felt like I still owed you the explanation even if it was ten years late."

He shook his head. "You didn't owe me an explanation, and I'm sorry that I made you feel like you did. It was your life and your decisions, and I wasn't a part of them, and that's okay."

"But it isn't. Eli, I want you to be a part of my life."

"I guess some of it was jealousy back in high school. But now? I don't know, I guess I thought I was more mature than that. I didn't think I was the kind of guy who hung on to a grudge from high school. You know, the loser who hates the quarterback for the rest of time."

I chuckled. "You're hardly that."

"I just wanted to know that whatever had come between us back then wasn't coming between us now. It felt like you had burned the bridges between us, and all this time later, I felt like it was happening again. But I never should have said that I didn't care."

I decided to take a risk and took one of his hands into both of mine. "I never meant to burn any bridges, but I realize that I did. I shut you out because of my own shame and guilt, and that wasn't fair to you. But I'm not burning any bridges now. In fact, I'm rebuilding the bridges if you'll let me."

He snorted. Eli actually snorted, then, I guessed feeling a bit embarrassed, said, "I'm sorry, I didn't mean to laugh, but that was so corny."

"Shut up," I said, though I couldn't stop the smile spreading on my own face.

He was still laughing. "Okay, okay, I'm sorry."

"I'm not shutting you out again. I don't want that distance to form again. I want us to fix what we broke."

He added his other hand to our intertwined hands. "Me, too."

"You're too important to me. Because of you, I see things differently now."

He furrowed his brow. "What do you mean?"

"I mean that I finally realized what I want in life, and I already have it. I was spending way too much time dwelling on the past and what I thought I wanted that I didn't see the great life in front of me. I don't want to move to Boston, Eli. I don't want to be in a city away from my family and away from everyone I love. I don't want to marry someone like Ryan who wants to go out to a new restaurant every weekend and attend corporate events. I want to stay in River Glen and be a teacher and get married and have kids. I want to be happy with who I am and stop wishing for something I'm not."

"Really?" Eli asked, a wide smile spreading rapidly on his face, and I liked that he seemed unable to contain it.

I nodded. "And I want you to be a part of that life."

Eli dropped my hands, and for a moment, I was afraid that I had said too much. Maybe Eli still only wanted to be friends. Maybe he was hoping we could go back to the way we were, not the way we had started to be. But then Eli reached up with both of his hands and slowly slid them up my neck to hold my face gently. His hands felt so warm on my chin, and I so enjoyed the way it felt. His thumb moved gently across my cheek, and he smiled at me, and with his smile, my whole body lit up.

"April, all I've ever wanted is you."

And before I could answer, he kissed me, not abruptly but suddenly, and it was the kind of kiss you just melt into. It felt just right, like somehow we'd always been this way, and yet it felt so brand new and exciting. My eyelids fluttered closed, and I sank into the feeling I'd been waiting for—the feeling of warmth of his lips on mine and his hands on my chin. I moved my hands to his lower back, and we stayed like that for awhile just enjoying how it felt to finally kiss each other. It felt like Eli's hands were made to touch my face, fitting perfectly around my cheeks and neck. Distantly, I was aware that we were kissing in the middle of our ten year high school reunion and everyone was probably staring, but unlike high school, I no longer cared what my classmates thought of me. I was happy, this was what I wanted, and I didn't care anymore about anything else.

Eli pulled back just slightly but kept his hands around my face and smiled. "I've always wanted to do that."

"You probably should have just done it. We could have saved a lot of time."

He laughed. "Oh sure, blame it on me."

"Clearly neither one of us knew what we wanted back then."

"At least we do now."

I glanced around the room and was surprised to find that fewer people than I thought had noticed us, but we'd definitely drawn some attention. I jutted my head in the direction of the big tree adorned with lights. "Should we join the reunion?" I asked. "I think the dancing has really picked up."

"Not embarrassed to dance under the tree with me anymore?"

"Actually, it sounds like the only thing I want to do right now."

He smirked. "The only thing?"

"Maybe one more thing."

This time I kissed him, and it was just as good as the first time. We had already fallen into a rhythm, and kissing Eli was unlike kissing anyone else. I didn't want to kiss anyone else for the rest of my life.

Eli said in a low voice just inches from my lips, "I love you, April. I always have."

"I love you, too, Eli."

And I thought that I always had, too, but I hadn't put it all together until now. I had spent so much time trying to force my life to fit into the box that I wanted for it that I couldn't see what was right in front of me. Eli had always been right in front of me.

Ten years ago, I wrote down goals for my life, and I had meant them at the time. I had thought that I knew exactly what I wanted, but things change, and the wonderful thing about growing up was finally knowing exactly what you wanted and being confident enough to go after it. On a "Ten Years from Now" fill-in-the-blank sheet, I never would have written being a high school teacher as a career, I wouldn't have pictured myself in River Glen, and Eli probably wouldn't have been featured as anything more than a friend. But tonight, as Eli led me by the hand to the tree in the park covered with lights to dance at our high school reunion, I decided that those kinds of lists were nothing more than fun. I had let one rule my life, and that just wasn't the way I wanted to live my life anymore.

Now when I looked ahead at the next ten years of my life, I recognized goals that I had for myself. I still wanted to get a PhD, but I also wanted a husband, kids, and a home. I wanted to raise a family, and I wanted to do that with Eli in his parents' house. I wanted to keep teaching and get better at it and coach Model UN and build those relationships with my students. I wanted my life to mean something not just to other people but to me. I knew that everything might not go the way I pictured it, but I wasn't scared of that anymore. The beauty in life was the discovery, and I welcomed the chance to explore the next phase of my life.

As Eli and I started swaying under the lights, he smiled at me and said, "Have I ever told you that you look beautiful in yellow?"

I smirked. "What happened to blue? I thought you said blue suited me."

Eli twirled me and pulled me back into his arms. "Any color you wear looks beautiful as long as I get to see you smile."

I smiled back at him. Eli didn't want to change anything about me, and I didn't want to change anything anymore either. I was a teacher who wore a yellow dress because it made me happy, and Eli saw the beauty in that. Ten years from now, I could only hope that we would still find the beauty in our lives together, whatever that might look like.

* * *

ACKNOWLEDGEMENTS

This is the first book I ever wrote (published or unpublished) that isn't young adult, and that was such a new experience. I had to change completely how I thought about writing a book, what genre conventions to follow, and how to picture my reader. This would have been a MUCH more difficult process without these people to thank.

Thank you to Lyssa from Booked Forever Shop for making sense of my confusing and sometimes contradictory requests to create this beautiful cover. I knew when I decided to write this story about Ms. Corwin from *Thank You for Applying* that I wanted to have you design the cover for the sake of consistency, but I continue to be thrilled by your work. Thank you for also assisting in the form of designing about half of the internal illustrations for this book.

Thank you to Kayla Tirrell for being someone who made me feel like I could write a romance novel. The ways that you generate ideas, write scenes, and push through challenges are inspiring, and I have so much respect for you as an author but, more importantly, as a friend. Thank you for entertaining my millions of questions about the romance genre that probably sounded stupid and for reminding me that in a romance novel, there have to be feelings. Reader, you'd be surprised how often I forgot that.

Thank you to my graduating class of 2012 at LCS. This idea first came to me after I attended our ten year high school reunion. I hadn't known what to expect from my high school reunion, but I was surprised by how familiar everything felt. I consider myself so grateful to have attended a high school that I loved so much that I even wanted to attend my reunion. I know how rare that can be. A big part of the reason I wanted to go to my reunion is because of all of you. You made our shared high school experience something memorable that brings a smile to my face and, apparently, even inspires me. I promise you that none of these characters are directly any of you!

A big thank you to everyone who played a role in my journey of becoming a teacher: my family, my friends, my teachers at BSBA and LCS, my professors at USF, and my earliest co-workers at CPCS. As a kid, I could only ever realistically imagine two careers for myself: teaching and writing. What a joy it is that I now get to do both. While April and I don't share many characteristics, the one we share is a deep love of the teaching profession. I'm grateful to have had too many people in my life who supported me that it would simply make my acknowledgements section too long to list all of you. Know that I think of you all regularly.

Thank you to every student I've ever taught and to those I'll teach in the future. My teaching career was always for all of you. April may have taken the long road to realizing that all she ever wanted was to teach, but I didn't: it was always for all of you from the start.

Thank you to Morgan Brownlee, Laina Strickland, Kristen Christensen, and Kelly Layne for buying every book, asking me to sign them, and cheering for me. You don't have any idea how much I appreciate you.

Thank you to my parents Brian and Sylvia who argue over which book I'll release next whenever I tell them the multiple ideas I'm considering. Some people think I do too much, but you never have. Thank you for reading every book I release pretty much immediately. Thank you to my sister Ashley for buying every book and for asking how best to support me. Starting up a career as an author isn't easy, and you all have made it feel possible.

ABOUT THE AUTHOR

When she's not writing books about teachers, she is one. An English teacher in Florida, Kristen Grafton is a Florida native with an MFA in Popular Fiction & Publishing and an MA in English Rhetoric. She was a triple major in college. She has an unhealthy obsession with her cats and Taylor Swift. She is also the author of the following YA novels:

Thank You for Applying
Line of Succession
The Waves at My Window

To learn more about Kristen Grafton, follow her on Instagram @kmgrafton1 and visit www.kristenmgrafton.com.